Bite Me!

Melissa Francis

HARPER TEEN
An Imprint of HarperCollinsPublishers

For my mother:
the strongest woman I know.
Thank you.

HarperTeen is an imprint of HarperCollins Publishers.

Bite Me!
Text copyright © 2009 by Melissa Francis
All rights reserved. Printed in the United States of America.
No part of this book may be used or reproduced in any manner whatsoever without written permission
except in the case of brief quotations embodied in critical articles and reviews. For information address
HarperCollins Children's Books, a division of HarperCollins Publishers, 10 East 53rd Street, New York, NY
10022.
www.harperteen.com

Library of Congress Cataloging-in-Publication Data
Francis, Melissa McKenzie.
    Bite me! / by Melissa McKenzie Francis. — 1st ed.
        p.   cm.
    Summary: AJ, a teenage vampire, hides her identity from her new stepfamily—among which is her ex-
boyfriend—and investigates the secrets of her heritage.
    ISBN 978-0-06-143098-5
    [1. Vampires—Fiction.   2. Stepfamilies—Fiction.   3. High schools—Fiction.   4. Schools—
Fiction.]   I. Title.
PZ7.F84685Bi   2009   2009001403
[Fic]—dc22   CIP
                                                                                                    AC

Typography by Jennifer Rozbruch
09 10 11 12 13   LP/RRDH   10 9 8 7 6 5 4 3
❖
First edition

Chapter 1

My mother's wedding day.

I should be thrilled she's getting hitched to the man of her dreams. And don't get me wrong; part of me is truly happy for her. Mr. Fraser—I mean, Rick—is a great guy. I like him. A lot.

But I like his oldest son, Ryan, even more.

In twenty minutes I was supposed to walk down the aisle, but I couldn't pull myself out of the old tree house. This was *our* spot. Every day for five months Ryan and I had met here after school. We'd do homework, watch the sunset, and look at the stars through the hole in the ceiling. It was the first place we kissed.

And now we wouldn't be kissing anymore. Because he

was going to be my brother.

I glanced down at my watch to gauge my time.

In theory, we now had nineteen minutes left before our parents did the deed. It would probably take me five minutes to track him down, which would give us approximately fourteen minutes for one last make-out session.

Of course, that equation didn't factor in travel time to and from the tree house. Which would probably only give us about three minutes of actual face time.

Would it be worth it?

Hell, yeah.

The rope ladder creaked and Ryan called out, "AJ? Are you up here? They're looking for you in the house."

My heart dipped. Of course he would know where to find me. I smiled.

"Hey," I said. "I was just saying good-bye to an old friend." *And daydreaming about playing one more round of tongue twister with you.*

"We don't have to say good-bye," Ryan said. He held out his hand and I accepted it. He pulled me into his arms and wrapped me up in a hug.

I could hear his heart racing. Or was that mine?

He framed my face with his hands and pulled me closer to him.

I sighed into Ryan as our lips met. It startled me when a tear slipped free and trailed down my cheek.

My heart and head were fighting. I had wanted this, but now the kiss made my chest hurt even more. "No." I forced myself to push him away.

Hurt shimmered in Ryan's eyes.

"I'm sorry," I said as I headed toward the door.

I climbed down the ladder, and Ryan followed just as the band began to play. We walked silently toward the outdoor wedding. I guiltily scanned the small crowd of people to see if anyone knew we had just been kissing in the tree house. Only one person seemed even remotely interested in where we had been, and that was Lindsey Rockport.

She shot me a look and then gazed adoringly at Ryan.

Well, he was free now. She could have him.

My chest ached at that thought, but really, what could I do?

I glanced at Ryan one last time before I took my place next to my mom. The look on his face broke my heart.

Maybe that kiss hadn't been worth it after all.

It was a fairly cool evening for August in Mississippi as I stood next to Mom trying to concentrate on the ceremony.

I took in the details of her pale pink dress, trying my hardest not to look at Ryan while our parents spoke of love and forever.

Her gown was a simple slip that sparkled in the sunlight. Unfussy and elegant. Just like the woman who wore it. Unfortunately, there was nothing else simple about this wedding. At least not for Ryan and me.

I wasn't mad at Mom for marrying Rick—how could I be mad at her for finding the love of her life—but I was heartbroken. And while today may be her happiest day, it was one of my worst. How could she expect me to just switch the *way* I love Ryan? Did she think changing her name would be like waving a wand that would magically help me change my feelings for him from boyfriend to brother? Especially now that we'll be under the same roof?

I felt Ryan's dark brown eyes burning into me, and I tried to be discreet as I glanced over to where he and his brothers were standing up for their dad. I hoped he wouldn't catch me.

But I was busted.

My face warmed under his scrutiny and my heart skipped a beat.

Breathe.

Totally unfair. This time last week we were cuddled up in our tree house, getting our groove on. Okay, not really. But finally, after five months of dating, I had let Ryan have a little boob action. And we even toyed with the idea of some under the zipper action, until his stupid younger brother, Rayden, poured a metaphorical bucket of cold water on that idea when he barged in to tell us our parents were getting married.

"Oh my God! You're feelin' up our sister!" he'd said with a cackle. "We are officially a Mississippi cliché. Awesome."

"Get out, Raytard!" Ryan had yelled, chucking a pillow at the fourteen-year-old's head.

It had been hard finding out that we were being yanked apart as a couple but would be glued together as a family. I had always imagined Ryan in my future. But I had thought we would grow old together, not grow *up* together.

So here I stood with my two sisters in the backyard of the antebellum mansion our melting-pot family would call home, wearing my pretty dark pink sundress and staring across at my new "brothers" (the oldest of whom I still wanted to jump, by the way) while our parents vowed to love each other for eternity.

I wonder if Mr. Fraser—er, Rick—realized that eternity was not just a metaphor in our case.

After all, vampires tend to live for centuries.

"God, AJ, you look good enough to eat," Ryan whispered in my ear as we passed through the buffet line.

The hair on my nape stood at attention. As always, my senses were in constant overdrive when it came to Ryan Fraser. It was bad enough that I couldn't just turn around, bite him, and make him mine the way we undead used to do. No, we were *civilized* now. No more barbaric pillaging.

Which was a shame. Sometimes that boy's neck just needed a nibble.

The thought of not being able to kiss Ryan every day from this point forward was pure hell. Too bad I couldn't rewind time and get those nineteen minutes before the wedding back.

Breathe.

"I'm dying. How are we gonna be in the same house without touching?" he said, picking up a roll. "Do you realize our rooms are across the hall from each other? I don't think I can do this. We could meet in the tree house every day just like before—"

Tempting. So very tempting.

"Nobody said it would be easy." I sighed as he lightly stroked the backward S-shaped birthmark on my neck, sending chills down my spine. "But we don't have much of a choice. Our parents have already threatened us within an inch of our lives."

Actually, Momma's exact words to me were, "Ariel Jane, if you so much as look at that boy with fangs in your eyes again, I'll bite you myself. He's your brother now. Besides, you haven't learned to control your instincts, and they can't know the truth about us yet."

Ryan and I had started dating in the spring of our junior year—more than a month before our parents did. So it was totally unfair that we had to take a backseat to them. Especially with so little warning. Even now, looking at Ryan, my insides did this weird molten goo thing, and my heart fluttered like hummingbird wings.

But Momma was right about the whole control thing. I almost blew it last week when Ryan took my bra off. I was kissing his neck when he brushed his palm against my breast. My fangs popped out, nicking his skin. I nearly went old school on him when the scent of his blood hit me.

Then he groaned . . . and let's just say that up until

that moment, I'd never really understood the term "blood-lust."

"We could risk it," he whispered.

I grabbed a glass of ginger ale punch and turned to face Ryan, my cheeks warm with the memory of his touch. I hated this. Especially since I was so tempted to give in and go for it. But I couldn't. Momma depended on me, and sneaking around behind her back would be disrespectful to the family. Family first, she always said. And now Ryan was a part of that family.

My mind drifted back to the tree house. As much as I wanted those nineteen minutes back, I knew the moment had passed and we had to move on.

The air whooshed from my lungs. "No matter how tempting it is, we can't. And that's the end of it," I said.

"Why? Because *Mommy* said so?" Ryan asked.

Oof! Nice punch below the belt, bubba. I spun around to face him, heat blazing my cheeks. "You want to do this?" I asked. "You want to be together no matter what?"

His eyes lit up. "More than anything," he answered, a little breathless.

"Fine. Let's do it. But we're not going to sneak around like we're doing something wrong. We're not going to start off by lying. After the honeymoon we'll just tell them straight up we can't do the sib thing. We won't be allowed to stay here anymore, I'm sure, so we can move out. I'll get a job waiting tables somewhere. Maybe your dad will let you work for him. If you want us to be together, then we'll be together. I'm all in. Are you?"

Ryan paled and stepped back a little. "Um," he stammered.

My heart cracked. Sure, I was bluffing, but part of me had hoped he would say "Yes!" and that we could start making plans toward the growing old together part of my dream. I sighed. "Yeah. That's what I thought. This hurts me, too, Ryan, but I don't see that we have a choice."

And boy did that suck. No pun intended.

"There's always a choice, AJ. You just always *choose* to be the good girl," Ryan said bitterly.

"Then let's tell our parents and run away. And there's nothing 'good girl' about that option," I snapped. I hated being labeled the good girl.

What I hated even more? He was right.

I had spent my entire seventeen years doing my best to be a normal kid. Good attitude, great grades, super sportsmanship, never missing curfew, and winning all the Miss Congeniality awards on earth. Okay, not really, but if there was a Miss Congeniality award here in Valley Springs, I'd totally win it.

Overcompensating for being a vampire was hard work.

I hated knowing that if I grew too angry, too frustrated, or too emotional in any way, my fangs might just pop out. I drank blood disguised as vegetable juice at every meal. What other teenager did that? And honestly, I was doing more than hiding—I was denying. I hated everything about being different, so I did anything I could to appear normal.

Now I needed to be resolved in my decision to put family first and give Ryan a little shove away. I swallowed, trying to dislodge the lump in my throat. The very thought of pushing Ryan away had tears burning my eyes. But maybe if Ryan were mad at me, he would leave me alone.

And then maybe it would be a little bit easier for *me* to get over him.

"You need to move on," I said, regretting the words the moment I uttered them. "Look, there's Lindsey Rockport. She's been giving you cow eyes all night long. I know she's had a crush on you since last year. Should be easy pickings."

"Fine. You want me to move on? I'll move on," he said as if accepting a challenge.

Smooth move, Metamucil.

I found my seat at the family table and watched my thirteen-year-old twin sisters, Ana and Ainsley, practice their cheerleading routine for a group of very interested preteen boys. Ryan sulked his way over to sit next to his brothers, Rayden and Oz. At ten, Oz was now the youngest of both families.

Wow. Three blond-haired sisters and three dark-haired brothers. Throw in a housekeeper and we'd be the goddamned Brady Bunch.

Of course, I don't think Marcia, Marcia, Marcia ever let Greg feel her up.

And I'm pretty certain they weren't bloodsuckers.

But what do I know?

"Let me help you with that," I said to the stout little redheaded woman carrying a tray of dirty dishes to the kitchen.

She smiled. "Thank ye, dearie, but I have been cleanin' up after this family for a long time now. But you're sweet to ask," she said in her thick Scottish accent.

I recognized her then. "You're Aunt Doreen, right?

Ryan's great-aunt?" I picked up another tray of dishes off the table and hoisted it to my shoulder with a grunt. It was a lot heavier than I thought. Or maybe Doreen was a lot stronger than she looked.

"I am," she said, pointing to a table in the carport. "Just leave that tray there. I'll get to those in just a few minutes. Rick has always said the nicest things about you. I can see he wasna foolin'. Those lads are good boys, but it takes a cattle prod to get them to help with anything."

"Well, I'm the oldest in the family, and with Mom being a single parent and a doctor, I learned early on to help out. Just easier that way."

"Such a sweet child. Go back out there and enjoy the rest of the party. Leave the mess for the adults to clean up."

I made my way around to the backyard and found the band was packing up. A few guests lingered in the garden, but the party was pretty much over. Lindsey and her best friend, Meredith Taylor, were putting away their instruments. I watched as Ryan approached them mumbling something under his breath. Meredith blushed like he was a celebrity, while Lindsey shot me a suspicious glance over her French horn.

I moved a little closer to pick up a napkin that had

blown off the table. The fact that I could hear their conversation just happened to be a bonus.

Ryan plucked a daisy from the centerpiece on the table and tucked it behind Lindsey's ear.

"You going to O'Reily's party tonight?" he asked her.

Lindsey shrugged and said, "Why would I go to a bonfire in the summer?"

Meredith rolled her eyes. "Because they're fun."

"I guess. If you call standing around a fire in ninety-degree heat fun." Lindsey shrugged again. And, just like she always did, with one statement she sucked the conversation dry. She was so clueless.

"Aren't you going with Peppermint Perfect over there?" she asked.

I should've given her more credit. Lindsey Rockport wasn't nearly as clueless as I thought.

Ryan laughed and my heart sank. "Nope. We broke up. The parents didn't think it was a good idea for me to date my sister. Besides, we had already cooled off. The family thing was just a good excuse to end it without drama."

Ouch. Now I know what being gutted felt like. Ryan just filleted me like a fish. What had I been thinking sending him straight into the arms of Lackluster Lindsey?

Of course, I *had* hoped she'd shoot him down. By

the googly eyes she was giving him, I should've known better.

Lindsey was pretty, in a plain sorta way. She played French horn in the school band (as well as at weddings) and was the yearbook editor. She had dark hair, dark eyes, and a petite build, so she had all the right ingredients to be cute. But she totally needed to drop by the Estée Lauder counter at Dillard's.

The real problem with Lindsey wasn't her looks—it was her ability to suck the life out of a person with just one conversation. She's a total Debbie Downer—no matter what's going on, she sees the dark cloud, not the silver lining. A one-on-one with Lindsey generally left me feeling more soulless than even a vampire should.

Not that I don't have a soul. I do. We vamps have evolved over time into a "living" undead. My own—very unscientific—explanation is that some of the original vampires began to mate with the humans they loved instead of biting them. Eventually, babies were born with vampire traits. Now we breathe, sleep, love, hate, eat, age (well, not like humans age, but we do eventually wrinkle), and take our daily dose of hemoglobin from a glass. And that whole sensitivity to light thing? *So* last century.

Apparently another thing we feel? Jealousy.

I don't even know why Ryan bothered asking Lindsey to the bonfire when he wasn't going. Our parents had asked us to stay home tonight to help the younger sibs acclimate to their new home since the parentals were going to Memphis for their wedding night. And we had *both* promised we would.

It was downright mean of Ryan to lead Lindsey on that way.

I couldn't watch Ryan swing and miss with his faux attempt to "move on" with Lackluster Lindsey. As I turned away I heard Lindsey say, "Maybe I could give tonight's bonfire a shot. Especially since Peppermint Perfect won't be there. She's not coming, is she?" Lindsey asked in a voice so fake and sweet that *I* could taste the saccharine.

"No. She's staying home to babysit like a good little girl. It'll be just you and me."

My stomach roiled. What had I done? I couldn't be angry and I honestly shouldn't be hurt. I knew he was lashing out at me. But his words felt like poison darts. I blinked back the tears that were burning my eyes.

There was no need for me to torture myself any longer. Besides, I needed to finish unpacking my room.

We'd started moving stuff over here earlier in the week, but tonight would be our first night in the new house. I'd been dreading the thought of unpacking all my stuff and putting my bedroom together, so I was a bit surprised to walk in and find everything had been done for me. All my stuff had been unpacked and set up for me just like it was in my former house. Even the walls were the same pale yellow. A vase of fresh daisies sat on my bedside table, and my white cat was curled up at the foot of my bed.

Maybe we did have a maid after all.

"What do you think about all this, Spike?" I asked, scratching my purring cat behind his ears.

No answer. I bet if I were a teenage witch he'd talk to me.

I found my favorite cut-offs and fitted tank and quickly changed. It was only nine o'clock. I really wanted to go to O'Reily's, but since that was out of the question, I thought I'd explore the house a little.

My cell phone rang.

"Hey," my best friend, Bridget, said. "Have you gotten kinky with your new brother yet?"

"Shut up, Bridge. I suppose you're headed to O'Reily's tonight?"

"Not without you."

"Um. Yeah. About that—I promised Mom I'd stay with the kids tonight. I don't suppose you'd consider ditching the bonfire and hanging out with me instead?" I asked.

"I can't believe you're staying in on the last night of summer."

"I don't have a choice, Bridge. Mom asked me."

"There's always a choice," Bridget said, echoing Ryan. "I'll come over for a little while, but I'm not skipping entirely. I'm finally going to let Grady notice me tonight."

"I wondered when you were going to instigate Project Grady. See ya in a few."

We hung up and I headed downstairs.

There were still a few boxes littering the foyer, but overall, the house was mostly put together. I walked through the main living area where Oz and the twins were playing Xbox.

"Have you guys seen Ryan?" I asked, hoping they knew exactly where he was so I could avoid him. Even though I was mad at Ryan, I still got all juiced up around him. I couldn't afford any alone time with him. Especially in this big house with lots of hidden nooks and crannies.

"Yeah, he and Lindsey left about ten minutes ago."

That stopped me in my tracks.

"Oh."

Good God. I really *was* jealous. Hadn't I just pushed him to ask her? It's not like I could be with Ryan myself. And I *was* trying to avoid him. But I really didn't like the thought of that cesspool of negativity giving him . . . French lessons.

It's nothing, AJ. He's just trying to make you eat your words. Besides, he's your brother now, remember?

I walked into the massive bright orange kitchen to wait for Bridget. There was a note from Mom on the counter.

AJ AND RYAN,
THANKS FOR SACRIFICING YOUR LAST NIGHT OF SUMMER FOR THE FAMILY. WE PROMISE TO MAKE IT UP TO YOU.
MOM AND DAD

"You see your note then, dearie?" a familiar voice said from behind me.

I turned to see Aunt Doreen. She adjusted her nightcap—I didn't know people actually still wore nightcaps—and waddled over to the stove, where she put on a pot of water.

"Aunt Doreen, what are you doing here?" I asked. I guess I assumed Mom had asked us to stay because Aunt Doreen wouldn't be here.

"Well, right now I'm fixing m'self a spot o' tea," she said. "And then I plan to work the crossword puzzle while I drink me tea. And *then* I plan to go to bed."

"Oh, right. So, are you babysitting for Rick and Mom? Because I thought . . ."

"Heavens! I'm no babysitter. Not really. As you well know, I've lived with the Frasers since Moira died nearly ten years. You dinna think these lads could take care of themselves?" She scoffed. "With me nephew running his company and the wee lads in school? And for certain I planned to move on after the wedding, but yer mum's so busy at the hospital . . . so last night she asked if I would stay on. How could I say no to family?"

"Wow. So you're our Alice," I mumbled.

"Alice? No, darlin', it's Doreen. Are you peeked? I can whip up a concoction that will set you right in a jiffy—"

"No, ma'am. I'm fine. I've got to go. See you around."

I'm truly living a very Brady nightmare.

Chapter 2

The old black wall phone rang as Bridget walked into the kitchen.

"Hello?" I answered into the heavy receiver.

"Good, you're there," Mom said. "Rick and I are on our way back home. We barely got checked into our room before the hospital called," she said, clearly exasperated.

"So you're coming home?" I asked.

"Yes. It's an emergency. I'll be going to the hospital, but Rick will be home tonight. I just didn't want y'all to freak out when he comes in. We're leaving Memphis now."

"Okay. Oh, hey, Mom? Since Aunt Doreen's here and you're gonna be home, anyway, is it cool if I head to the bonfire now? I won't break curfew. I promise."

She sighed. "That's fine. I shouldn't have asked you to give up your last night of freedom. Have fun."

Smiling, I hung up the phone. "Mom and Rick are on their way home. Sucks being a doctor."

"Yup. But it doesn't suck for you," Bridget said.

"Let me update Aunt Doreen and then we can hit it. I'll drive."

We could see the bonfire from a mile away. I turned my Saturn down the winding, barely drivable path that led us through a patch of woods to the pasture. The field was peppered with other vehicles, haystacks, necking high school students, and the occasional roaming cow.

I pulled up on the other side of Grady Lincoln's big-ass truck and parked.

"Beer?" Bridget asked as she reached to the backseat, flipping open the ice chest.

"No, and you know that. By the way, you look hot tonight."

"Yeah, I know." She laughed and fluffed her dark auburn curls. "Is that Grady's truck?"

"Why do you think I parked here?"

"You're the best. Now, does this top say *you're the one*

for me or does it say *everyone has already had me?*"

Not that anyone had *had* either one of us. Got to watch out for false advertising.

She wore a shimmery white button-down that was tapered at the waist, but only two buttons were fastened.

"Button one more button at the top, but leave your belly button ring showing. For whatever reason, guys dig that."

"Gotcha."

She made the adjustments, got out of the car, and strutted over to Grady. That six-foot-four ballplayer was putty in her hands the moment she said hello.

I opened the cooler, and for a brief moment thought about grabbing a beer, then got smart and took a Coke instead.

Alcohol might be a downer to most people, but not to vampires. Especially if you don't have control over your instincts. And clearly, after last week's reaction with Ryan, I don't.

They also say that the purer your lineage, the greater the effects. I have a human grandmother, but mostly, my genetic stock is all vampire. Which means I don't need my senses any keener than they already are.

So I don't bother with the booze. I get high on life . . .

(ha!) and occasionally a bloodsicle or two (which are surprisingly tasty).

I joined Bridget and Grady, who were already making goo-goo eyes at each other. Hank Fellows and John Turner, two of Valley Springs, Mississippi's finest football players, sat on the tailgate of Grady's truck with road-pops in their hands.

"Mad Dog? Dudes, you gotta stay away from the malt liquor."

"Says she who doesn't drink," Hank said, nudging John in the side with his elbow. They both laughed like it was the funniest thing ever. That's when I noticed the joint.

I just rolled my eyes and stepped away from them. I couldn't get high for the same reason I couldn't drink. And since I wasn't sure what the secondhand smoke would do to me, I figured it was best to keep as far away from it as possible.

"See ya later, Sister Christian," John said with a snort as I walked away. I turned around, flashed them my most charming smile, and gave them the finger—in stereo.

"Nice." They both laughed.

I stepped over to the bonfire and left Bridget to her work.

"Hey, AJ," Noah James said, approaching the fire. "You ready for Monday?"

Noah was a soccer player, like me. He was a few inches taller than my five foot seven, with blond wavy hair and baby blues that would melt ice caps. I'd always had a little crush on him, but he was usually attached at the groin to Twittany Talbot.

I eyed him with appreciation. Yeah, there were worse things in this world to look at.

"Is anyone really ready for school to start?" I asked with a laugh. "Where's Tiffany?"

"We split over the summer. I finally woke up one day and realized how annoying she really was."

"Took you long enough." I grinned.

"Yeah, well, she wasn't nearly as aggravating when she was sitting on my lap." He waggled his eyebrows at me and took a pull off his beer. "I hear your mom and Ryan's dad got hitched today. That's gotta be weird for you guys. Or maybe just beneficial?"

"Not beneficial anymore. We split, too. The parentals made us."

"Oh."

A thick slice of silence stretched between us as we sipped our drinks and pretended not to be thinking about the fact we were both single, and it was the last Saturday before school started, and how fun it might be to celebrate our last night of freedom by laying into each other tongue deep. I mean, I had it bad for Ryan, but he was off limits. That didn't mean I had to take myself off the market, right?

Besides, he was clearly moving on and so should I.

"Oh. My. God," I heard Bridget say behind us. "No fucking way."

"You sing in the church choir with that mouth?" I laughed and turned to see what had her panties in a bunch.

Ryan was helping Lindsey Rockport out of his Jeep. And she stood there looking up at him with Bambi eyes and a Barbie smile.

"What's he doing here? With Lindsey? She's nothing but a big ball of hate wrapped up in a pint-size body. And is she *smiling*?" Bridget asked.

"Yeah, I think she is."

Ryan's gaze caught mine, and then he leaned down and kissed Lindsey on the neck, never breaking our stare.

A trill of giggles floated from her mouth to my ears. My head burned, and every molecule of my body ached to reach over and scratch her face off, then fang Ryan Fraser until his blood ran dry.

Jealous much?

A familiar tingle in my mouth warned me to settle down. I licked my lips and took a deep, calming breath, hoping to regain control over my fangs. This wouldn't be a good time for them to make a sudden, unwanted appearance, you know?

I'd like to see me try to explain that. "Oh, sorry about the fangs. Yeah, I'm a vampire, but don't worry, we've evolved."

"You okay?" Bridget asked.

"Fine. I'm fine. He's my brother now—remember? Besides, at the reception, I'd very clearly told him to move on. Hell, I even suggested he move on with Lindsey. I guess he thought that was a good idea." I tried to stamp down the giant green monster before it showed up in full force and made the Incredible Hulk look like an Oompah Loompah.

"I thought you might need this," Noah said, handing me a beer.

"She doesn't drink," Ryan said as he and Lindsey approached. "She doesn't do anything that breaks the rules. What *are* you doing here, anyway?" he asked me. "I thought you were home playing Nanny McPhee," he said.

I decided to ignore his question. If he had been home, he would know why I was here. "It's not about the rules, Ryan. It's about respect. That's probably a hard point for you to grasp, I know."

"Nope. Not at all. The point is: Ariel Jane Ashe equals status quo." He rolled his eyes and turned to Noah. "Good luck unlocking that chastity belt, Sport. She'll have to get written permission first." He chuckled, but it was cold and hollow.

His words dug at me. Like I wasn't already hurting. Like this was easy for me. Did he think I could just turn my feelings off like I would a suck-ass movie?

"Nice, Ryan. Real nice." I grabbed Noah's hand.

"You know, I think tonight is a night of firsts. Now, which rule should I break first? I think I'll start with the beer and then I'll finish with you, if you're up for it."

Noah's smile was all dimple as he handed me a beer. "I was hoping you'd say that."

He draped his arm around me, pulling me to him, and a fist squeezed my heart even as my belly did a little flip.

As we walked away I glanced over my shoulder to make a face at Ryan (because I'm mature like that), but he wasn't paying one bit of attention to me or my dramatic exit. Instead, he was wrapped up in Lindsey's arms as they slow danced and made out to some stupid Ne-Yo song.

I put the beer to my lips, closed my eyes, and drained the can like it was water. With that one gulp I washed away Dudette Do-Right and welcomed Little Miss Deviant.

"Damn!" Noah said, stretching the four-letter word out into two syllables. "For someone who doesn't drink, you sure put a hurtin' on that beer."

"Yeah. You got another?" I asked, knowing it was a mistake but not really giving a rat's ass.

It hurt, seeing Ryan with Lindsey. Even though I pretty much had pushed him into her arms, part of me had thought he would've at least pined a little bit first.

I glanced over at Noah as he opened his ice chest and took out two more beers, then reached behind the seat of his truck and pulled out a rolled-up blanket, tucking it under his arm.

I'm sure I didn't appear to be pining any, either. But couples hook up and break up all the time. What better way to move on than with someone else?

Noah handed me the beer, wrapped his big warm hand around mine, and said, "Let's find someplace we can be alone."

"Yeah." I needed to get away. The beer worked fast.

My senses were already opening up, and I could hear all the conversations, and music, and moaning, and giggling. A cow mooed in the distance, but it sounded like it was on my lap.

I was a little nervous about the private time in the woods with Noah. I had no intention of doing more than making out with him, but suddenly my skin was buzzing, my heart was racing, and my mouth was as dry as sand. I'd always had a slight crush on Noah, but for some reason, tonight was different. Everything was heightened and I wasn't sure if it was because of the beer, my hurt over Ryan . . . or just because Noah was really hot.

Maybe it was a dangerous combination of all three.

I took another big drink, trying to quench my thirst and tamp down the desire that had begun to curl its way through my system.

I inhaled deeply, and the scent of lust slammed into me like a crashing wave. My heart strummed to a faster staccato, my breathing hitched up a notch, and my insides started melting into a big puddle of horny.

And he hadn't even kissed me yet.

Wow. Drinking might have been a really bad idea.

Noah led me to a small clearing in the woods. The trees muffled the sounds to a bearable level, but my skin still buzzed when he touched me. And my heart hadn't slowed yet.

It was disconcerting how quickly my body was responding to the atmosphere and smells around me. No matter how much I wanted to pout and wail about Ryan, all I could think about was how many different ways I could rip Noah's clothes off his back.

I watched Noah kick away some acorns and rocks as he spread out the red and black plaid blanket. He was wearing a pair of tattered jeans that were frayed at the bottom and a tight olive green T-shirt that sported a super sexy picture of James Dean. When he bent over to smooth the blanket, I caught a glimpse of his paisley boxers poking out of a slash just beneath his back pocket.

My mouth tingled and my fangs popped out, slicing into my lower lip.

"Ow!" I cried, covering my mouth with my hand. I touched my tongue to my lip and a roaring need burst inside me. Blood.

I wanted blood.

Even though I'd had more than enough today, I found myself compelled to bite Noah.

"AJ? You okay?" Noah asked, turning to look at me.

"I bit my lip," I mumbled from behind my hand. I still

hadn't been able to retract my fangs. I closed my eyes to concentrate.

Focus on the white.

Mom had taught us a control exercise when we were kids. Vampires don't fully mature until after thirty, which means that although we can learn to somewhat manage our instincts, we probably won't be in full command of them until then. I've never been sure why thirty is the magic number. It seems a little late for puberty, but I guess thirty is actually a drop in the age bucket when you live for hundreds of years. Anyway, until vampires have control of their power, premature fangulation is always a concern.

Like, um, now.

Focus.

The darkness behind my eyelids faded to gray, then to white. I steadied my breathing as I concentrated on the bright emptiness. I counted to ten, never wavering from the blank canvas.

After what seemed like hours, I felt the incisors slide back into place.

When I opened my eyes Noah was standing just inches away.

"That must've hurt. Let me take a look," he said, gently cupping my chin in his hand. He angled my face and rubbed his thumb across my bottom lip. "I have just the cure for that nasty scratch," he said.

It happened in slow motion, just like in the movies. Noah leaned over until his face was just a breath away from mine.

I hesitated at first. Something in the back of my mind warned me that this could be a very bad idea. But a picture of Ryan with Lindsey flashed through my mind, and jealousy roared to life, drowning out any warning bells that had been ringing.

I closed my eyes, partly to ready myself for the kiss and partly to focus and keep my incisors parked.

Noah's lips were soft, as I had imagined they would be. At first, the kiss was just a timid touch of his lips to mine. He brushed his thumb along my cheek to my neck. Then he grabbed the back of my head and kissed me again, this time with more intent.

His mouth coaxed mine open. When our tongues touched, my skin sparked and the white screen behind my eyelids grew as bright as the halogen lamps in science class.

My arms snaked around his neck, and I nearly scaled up his torso, trying to push my body closer to his.

My skin itched to be touched, and my senses opened to

every smell and sound in the forest. Crickets, owls, bats—mushrooms, pine, moss; all of it earthy, all of it strangely sexy.

As if Noah read my mind, his hand found its way under my top. Goose bumps trailed after his touch as he softly caressed my belly, then my waist, then around to my lower back.

Noah took his time, working his way up my spine, then to my shoulder. He slid the spaghetti strap down and worked his mouth down my neck. Then he scooped me up in his arms and laid me down on the blanket.

Chapter 3

"I'm glad we're finally hooking up," Noah whispered into my neck as he sprinkled my bare shoulder with kisses. "The timing was never right before."

"It's right now," I said. Actually, I think I purred, because he flushed and his aura lit up like a fire.

I reached up and pulled his mouth back to mine. My senses were in hyperdrive, and every touch and every kiss felt like a thousand. A flickering thought of Ryan drifted through my mind and my heart splintered, but I stamped down the guilt with another hungry kiss.

Nothing but untamed lust for this boy I'd only been mildly attracted to before. My body practically acted on its own, and I had to fight the tingling in my gums to keep my fangs banked.

I want to bite him.

The thought drifted casually through my head as everything inside me cried out to take him, bite him, and make him mine. Noah's finger brushed the pink lace of my bra strap, and the white behind my eyes flashed red.

Noah's mouth trailed from my neck to my shoulder; suddenly the red behind my eyes brightened, like a fire consuming a pile of dry leaves.

My incisors exploded from my gums, and I growled in pain and frustration. I licked Noah's neck first, knowing my saliva would numb the area like Lidocaine while my fangs were out. Thank God it was just normal spit when my fangs were banked. Otherwise I'd never be able to feel my tongue and that would just be weird.

When my tongue touched his skin, I tasted sweat and hunger and it filled me, driving me forward without thought. With Ryan, I had been aware and able to regain control. Did the booze make it different with Noah? Whatever the reason, I was spiraling forward on instinct alone. Aware but unable to control my desire . . . my powers.

It was like thousands of years of vampire history and instincts were mushrooming inside me and I couldn't do a damn thing about it.

Strangely, the world around us silenced, except for one lone voice.

Go ahead. Taste him. It's what you were born to do.

I hesitated while the voice in my head wrestled with my gut. Was that my voice? Where had that come from?

Noah ran his hand up my thigh and the voice tempted me again.

Just. One. Taste.

The tips of my fangs touched his neck, and my mouth actually watered, like a wolf drooling over a fresh kill.

"AJ! Where are you?" Bridget's voice broke through my red fog. "AJ! I have a surprise for you!" It sounded like she was standing over us, but when I opened my eyes, we were alone.

Then Ryan's voice filled my head. "AJ? You won't believe who's back," he yelled.

"Shhhh," Noah said, pinning me to the ground. "If we stay quiet, maybe they'll give up and go away."

They were close enough that Noah could hear. What the hell was I doing? I closed my eyes and tried to focus. I forcefully pushed the red away and concentrated on white. I needed the white. I'd never been in a situation like this before; I had been a millisecond away from biting Noah.

And I had no idea what biting him would do.

What if I was venomous? Could one bite change him?

Finally—the red began to slowly fade to white. I sighed with relief when my gums opened and my fangs disappeared.

"Over here," I yelled back. I reached down and pulled my bra strap back to my shoulder. "I'm so sorry, Noah. This was a mistake. I'm not ready."

I tried to wriggle away, but he tightened his hold.

"You seemed ready enough just a few seconds ago," he snapped. "I never pegged you as a tease."

"And I never pegged you as a sleaze," I retorted, finally pushing him off me. I grabbed my shirt from the ground and shrugged into it. "Bridget, Ryan! Can y'all hear me?"

No answer. I had no idea how close they were because my hearing was still super sensitive. But Noah had heard them, too, so they couldn't be too far away.

We both stood. Noah huffed as he pulled his jeans up. Things had progressed a lot further than I'd realized. Thank God for Bridget and, as much as it pained me to admit it, Ryan.

I heard footsteps, so I took a step in the direction of the sound.

"We're not finished," Noah growled, grabbing my arm. "You wrote me a check and now you're going to cash it."

He crushed me against him, forcing my hand to his crotch as his mouth half-swallowed my face. Red glowed bright in my head. Fear and anger shot through me and I struggled to pull free. Panic burned my throat, and my gums started to tingle.

I tried to stop them but couldn't. My fangs forced their way out and sliced into Noah's tongue. He screamed and pushed me away.

"You bit me! You bitch!"

"You forced me to touch you. You're lucky that's all I did," I muttered from behind my hands. But there was no need. My fangs had already receded like good little teeth.

Bridget and Ryan both called my name again, but this time I could tell they were close.

"Over here!" I yelled.

Bridget raised her eyebrows, her eyes darting from me to Noah as she approached. He had picked up his shirt and was using it to wipe the blood off his face.

"Um. Did we come at a bad time?" she asked.

"No, you came at the perfect time," I said. "I thought Ryan was with you."

"I'm here," Ryan said, his aura turning black when he

looked at Noah. But when Ryan looked at me, his brown eyes shined dark with pain, not anger.

"And I'm here, too," a once-familiar voice said as someone else stepped into my view.

"Malia?" I cried when the girl with Ryan came into focus.

I squealed as she ran over to me, and we danced around in a hug. Malia Gervase was our closest friend from childhood. Our freshman year, her parents died in a car accident, and she'd moved away to live on the coast with her grandmother. We'd kept in touch via email, text messages, and Facebook, but it just wasn't the same as live and in person.

"Long time no see, Noah," she said, giving him a look that could kill. She took my hands and gave me the once-over. "You are smokin' hot, my friend."

Malia was a good two inches taller than me. She'd obviously had a growth spurt since I'd last seen her. She'd also added a few blond highlights to her long straight brown hair and had gotten blue contacts to cover her iced-tea-colored eyes. It really worked for her.

She smiled wide, showing off her now brace-free teeth. "I wanted to surprise y'all," she said. "I just couldn't stand one more year in that crappy little wannabe town.

And after Katrina, we had to find somewhere permanent. It feels good to be back in a house without ten other family members."

"I can't think of a better surprise. Isn't it awesome, Bridge? We're a tripod again!"

"You're gonna regret this," Noah spat.

Crap. I had almost forgotten about Noah. He stood there bleeding and scowling. My senses were returning to normal, but I could still smell his rage.

"It's obvious the only thing that matters to you is helping little Noah park his Ark. Why don't you call Twittany? I'm sure she'll be happy to reopen her tunnel of love."

"Here," Bridget said. "Sounds like you need this more than I do." She handed him a beer.

He took the beer and drank it down in one long pull. Bridge, Malia, and I hooked arms and turned to walk away.

"You coming?" I asked Ryan.

"Not just yet," he answered.

"Don't be stupid, Ryan. He's not worth it."

"I'm sure he's not," Ryan said. "But it'll make me feel a helluva lot better."

Fine. Let them sort it out in testosterone. Ryan obviously wasn't in any mood to listen to reason.

"Wanna tell me what happened?" Bridget asked as she tugged me away from the boys' pissing contest.

"No, I just wanna catch up with Malia, then go home."

"Are you okay to drive?" Bridget asked. "I know you didn't drink much, but wow, you look a little wild-eyed."

"I'm fine. I didn't even finish the second beer, and that was a while ago. Besides, if that thing with Noah didn't sober me up, nothing will. C'mon, let's get out of here."

Chapter 4

The sound of feet pounding down the stairs echoed through the house, waking me from my dead sleep. The twins were laughing as Rayden screamed at them about staying out of his room, especially when he had his "Do not disturb" door hanger on. Poor kid. "Do not disturb," to the twins, was like an open invitation to snoop.

My head was still foggy. I barely remembered getting home. And I didn't remember going to bed at all.

I must've passed out right away, because I was still wearing last night's outfit. I slipped off my tank top and started to toss it on the floor when something on the shirt caught my eye.

Little dots of crimson were sprinkled on the shirt. Weird. Where did that come from? I glanced toward my bed and saw a larger red stain on my pillow. That's when I really started freaking out.

I rushed into my bathroom and sighed with relief when I saw the crusted blood around my nose. Generally, vampires only experience nosebleeds when we're overstuffed or overstressed. I hadn't had a nosebleed since I had overindulged on bloodsicles as a kid.

Since I was currently starving, I could rest easy knowing that I had *not* gone into a sleepwalking feeding frenzy and stuffed myself with hemoshakes.

Doreen's voice echoed after the slamming screen door. "Ye'll mind each other well, ye will! Stop this foolishness." I heard a pop, like a giant tree limb breaking. The twins squealed in unison.

I glanced out my bathroom window. Sure enough, a giant limb had broken off of a pine tree and crashed to the ground. Doreen and Rayden stood next to it, talking to each other. The twins were nowhere to be seen.

Disappeared, just like that. If I didn't know better, I'd think they'd inherited the rare trait of invisibility. Man, what I wouldn't give to have *that* power.

A knock sounded on my door, followed by my Mom's

lyrical Southern voice. "AJ? May I come in?"

It's not like I could fake being asleep. I mean, I could try, but the reality was, Mom knew I was awake. And probably, she knew something was bothering me, which was why she wanted to see me. I quickly washed my face, shrugged into my robe, and flipped over my stained pillow.

"C'mon in."

Mom closed the door behind her, walked over to my bed, and sat down, patting a place next to her. She was dressed in a pair of khaki shorts and a green polo that really brought out the green in her hazel eyes. We have the same wheat-colored hair, as do the twins. Today she sported a ponytail at the nape of her neck.

Mom has always looked young for her age. We've even been mistaken for sisters before. Not that she's old. But right now, she even looked a good ten years younger than thirty-eight. We've always been more like friends than anything else. It's hard being a vampire and having almost nobody to talk to—so we talk to each other.

"What's up?" I asked.

"My spidey-sense is telling me something's wrong with my number-one girl," she said.

I smiled weakly and sat next to her, putting my head on her shoulder.

"I know this isn't easy," she said, wrapping her arm around me. "And I know it wasn't fair of Rick and me to just throw this at you guys. But, honestly, we thought it would be better than a long, drawn-out engagement. Especially with you and Ryan dating. We didn't want you two to get any more involved. A whirlwind wedding seemed like the easiest answer."

"Easy for you, sure. But not for me. Not for Ryan. Mom, I screwed up, and it's all your fault."

"How did you screw up? You and Ryan aren't still sneaking around, are you? You know, honey, there's a great big world out there and you're not the only person in it. Rick and I did what we thought was best for the family, and in the grand scheme of things, this is a small problem. I know not being with Ryan seems like the end of the world. But you're almost eighteen. There will be other boys. You'll see."

I sighed. "Well, there kinda already was another boy. And if you and Rick had waited—"

She stiffened. "What did you do, AJ? Did you have sex last night? Please tell me you were safe."

I had to laugh at this because my mom isn't like most other mothers. Besides the whole vampire thing, she's also a doctor. Actually, a lot of health care workers are vampires. Why do you think there's always a blood short-age? It's not because the donations aren't being made—it's because they're being cycled out to underground blood suppliers.

Anyway, Mom has never been one to shy away from sex talk. Since the sex thing and the vampire thing go hand in hand, it's just something that we grow up understanding. The longer we wait for sex, the better our control is—and the sooner we have sex, the more likely it is we screw up. (I guess that's really no different from regular teens, come to think about it.)

Mom *didn't* wait. She and my dad had this intense love affair and wound up pregnant with me. The marriage lasted ten years. Then the intensity faded and Dad moved on. We haven't seen him since.

So she's always preached the safe-sex thing. Not because of diseases. Vampires are generally immune to STDs and most illnesses. (We're made of some sturdy stock.) No, we have to avoid pregnancy until we're ready because, thanks to our old friend evolution, we also tend to be very fertile. And Mom knows good and well I'm not anywhere near being ready. What high school kid is?

"No, Mom. No sex. But I . . . kinda sorta drank last night."

"Ariel! I thought you were smarter than that. What happened?"

"Ryan was making out with Lindsey and I was so hurt, so I grabbed a beer and . . . everything was so intense. The smells, the sounds, the touches. I totally lost control. I was seeing red and no matter how hard I tried, I couldn't re-focus on the white. It was like nothing I'd ever felt before. And then my fangs descended. Mom, my teeth were on his neck when Bridget and Ryan called out for me and broke through my fog."

A tear rolled down my cheek. "Momma, I wouldn't have stopped if they hadn't been looking for me. I wouldn't have stopped." A sob escaped, and I buried my face in her chest while she held me and stroked my hair.

"Shh. It's okay, baby. The only thing that matters is that they got to you and you did stop."

She cupped my face in her hands and made me look her in the eyes. "You stopped. The boy is okay. You're okay. But AJ, you have to realize how serious this could've been. Do you understand?"

I nodded.

"Don't let this happen again. I know you're scared, and you should be. We've all had a close call at one time or another, but this one could've been avoided if you hadn't touched alcohol."

"I know." I sniffed. "It was stupid."

"Yeah. It was." Mom stood and gave me a gentle smile. "Once we get settled in here, you and I are going to start working on more control exercises. But for now, you need to stop dwelling on what could've happened. It won't change anything. So, as your doctor, I'm ordering you to put it out of your mind, at least for today. What do you say to some shopping in Memphis?"

Like I would ever turn down a trip to the mall.

"Sounds like a miracle cure. I'm in."

etail therapy was so good that I didn't even mind waking up at six o'clock the next morning. The first day of senior year. And now that Malia was back, our circle of three was complete. All was right in my world.

Except for the whole stepbrother / ex-boyfriend thing, and that disastrous make-out session with Noah. But really, did that stuff matter?

I think not.

The house was a big buzzing box of chaos. The twins had recruited Oz to assist them in torturing Rayden. Ana ran through the kitchen, holding a piece of paper that Oz had just handed her, while Ainsley stood in a kitchen chair holding Rayden's backpack over her head.

"Which one do you want more?" Ana asked a red-faced Rayden. "Your love note from Samantha Burk or your backpack?"

"I'll get them both," Rayden snapped. He turned to his little brother. "And I'll deal with you after school."

Oz's dark eyes went wide, and his freckles paled. Despite the hint of brotherly terror, he stuck to his guns. "C'mon, Ray, don't be such a sore loser just because you got outsmarted by two girls and your baby brother."

"That's enough," Rick said as he entered. He was dressed just as the big-time CEO of some fancy pots and pans company should be dressed—expensively. "Girls, give Rayden his stuff back, and Oz, you need to be careful. Remember what happened the last time you crossed the line with your brother?"

Oz frowned and nodded while Rayden smirked. "Yeah, Roscoe. Don't mess with me—unless you wanna wake up in a bed of spiders again—"

"That's enough, Rayden," Rick warned.

Spiders? I shuddered. I had to remember not to piss the little turd off. If he ever put spiders in my bed, I'd bite first, and worry about Mom later.

Ainsley climbed down from the chair and handed

Rayden his backpack, but Ana didn't move. She opened the note and started to read. "'My little love pumpkin . . .'"

"It doesn't say that!" Rayden said, lunging for Ana.

"Anastasia Simone Ashe, give him his letter," Mom said. She walked into the kitchen, squeezed Rick's hand, and gave him a quick kiss. "Nice suit," she said to Rick. Then she turned back toward Ana. "I mean it. Hand it over. You're going to have to mind your boundaries, young lady."

"But Mom—"

"But nothing. We discussed this. We expect there to be an adjustment time, but you need to do your part to expedite things. Make things smoother. And sneaking into your brother's room and pilfering his stuff is not the way to do it. Am I understood?"

Ana nodded with an appropriately remorseful look on her face. She walked over to Rayden and handed him the note. "Here you go, 'love pumpkin.'"

"She didn't call me that, you skinny twerp!" he growled.

"Okay, okay. That's enough," Rick said. "Where's Ryan? You guys are going to be late if you don't leave soon."

"He left already," Oz said, pulling his Pop-Tart out

of the toaster. "He was picking up his new girlfriend this morning. He said we could ride with AJ."

"He said that? He said he was picking up his girl-friend?" I asked.

"Yup. *And* he said he'd give me ten bucks if I made sure you got that message," Oz said with his mouth full.

Ryan was now officially on my shit list. Any guilt I had over my make-out session with Noah was gone. Well, any guilt associated with Ryan was gone. The whole "coulda-possibly-sucked-the-life-force-outta-the-boy" guilt was kinda hard to shake—even if he did turn into an asshole afterward.

"I'll give you twenty if you promise to knee him with all your might in the—"

"All right, AJ," Mom said, effectively cutting me off. "Now, there's no way you can take all the kids in your car, so I'll take Oz and the girls since their schools are on my way to the hospital. You can take Rayden. Okay?"

"Fine," I said, shrugging into my backpack and drain-ing the hemoshake cleverly disguised as a V8 that I'd brought downstairs with me. "Let's go, Ray. But you have to sit in the back, because I'm picking up Bridget."

"Bridget Craig?" he asked with a squeaky voice and stars in his eyes.

"Yeah." I grinned at him. "Don't even waste your time, kid. She's a senior, you're a freshman. That's the stuff dreams are made of."

"Sometimes dreams come true," he said.

Bridge got into the car, saw Rayden in the backseat, and asked, "Why'd you bring the boil along?"

"Because Ryan had to go pick up his 'girlfriend' this morning."

"What an idiot. You don't need him."

I wound our way through the neighborhood, hung a left on Park Street, took the next right on Highland, and drove a few more blocks to Valley Springs High, home of the fighting Rangers.

The parking lot was mostly full, but I found a space near the science building. And it wasn't even an illegal spot. Not really. Besides, I hate parking two blocks away in the overflow lot.

"I have practice after school today," I said to Bridget, ignoring Rayden as he got out of the car. "You can either catch a ride home with someone else or meet me at the soccer fields."

"Grady's gonna take me home," she said with a big grin.

"Oh, really?"

"You know it," Bridget said, wiggling her eyebrows. "Now, let's go. We look too cute not to make an impression."

We did look good. I had on a new jean skirt that was probably too short for dress code standards, but if anyone questioned it, I could fake my way out.

Rayden followed us like a lost puppy as we walked up the steps into the main building. I felt sorry for the kid. I remembered my freshman year, much to my dismay. It wasn't easy, especially if you didn't know anyone.

And since his brother had abandoned him, it really wouldn't be fair to leave him treading water in the ocean of high school sharks.

"C'mon," I said, motioning him up to walk with Bridget and me. "I'm gonna give you the one secret you need to survive. Be the BMOC, even if you're not. Act it. Hold your head up and don't say anything today, even if someone speaks to you. Use your face to communicate. If you do have to speak, use short sentences. No more than three words. Be cocky but don't overdo it. Got it?"

He nodded eagerly.

"Okay, see, don't do that. Don't be eager. When you need to answer yes, then you either raise your eyebrow and give the 'WTF' look, or you nod once. Curt and to the point. No more eager beaver."

He gave me a brisk nod. It wasn't great, but it was a start.

"Okay, good. Now go find your friends. But remember, the less you say, the more mysterious you are."

He nodded again and walked away.

"Seriously, you think that's gonna help him?" Bridget asked.

"Um, it can't hurt. Look at him. He's a walking goob."

"Ryan was a goob once, too. Remember?"

Yeah, I remembered. He was a total dweeb. His arms were longer than they should've been. He wore braces— always with bright green bands—which made it look like he'd just snacked on Kermit the Frog. But something happened that summer between our sophomore and junior year. I couldn't really articulate exactly how he was different, but I will tell you when he came to school that August, I nearly lost my virginity just dreaming about him.

"Maybe with my help, Rayden won't have to go through the awkwards like his brother did."

The halls were alive with noise and excitement. Most of the girls were dressed to kill, and all the boys looked like they needed a cold shower.

"Check that out," Bridget said, pointing down the hall. "He's so obvious."

There was Ryan with his arm around Lindsey. They were leaning against the lockers, laughing it up. If he was trying to make sure I got the picture—message received.

"I can't believe she's smiling again. This is like a world record for her."

"*I* was smiling when Ryan Fraser was *my* boyfriend," I said.

"Yeah, but you smile for other reasons, too. She smiles when someone else has a crappier day than she does."

"Some people just don't see the silver lining. And honestly, I feel sorry for her. She's his rebound. When he dumps her, she'll never think another positive thought again."

"Is that what Noah was to you, your rebound?"

"Of course. But the difference between me and Noah and Ryan and Lindsey is, I was also Noah's rebound. He's no more over Tiffany than I'm over Ryan."

"How is that better?" Bridget asked.

"I don't know, it just is. But none of that matters now, because Noah's not even a rebound anymore. He's a reject."

"You're gonna have to spill the beans about Saturday night sooner or later."

"I will. Later. I wonder if Malia's here yet." I took one last look down the hall at Ryan. This was gonna be hard. Every bone in my body wanted to reach out for him, but I knew it couldn't happen.

He was moving on, just like I'd told him to. Now it was my turn.

"She said she hadn't registered yet, so she's probably in the office. You wanna walk over to meet her?"

"No, we only have a couple of minutes before the bell. I can't be tardy on the first day. Where's your locker and who do you have for first period?" I asked.

"You're never tardy," she said, rolling her eyes. "First period is Mr. Phelps, Western Civ. And my locker is eight seventy-six."

"Cool. My locker is eight ninety-seven, and I have Advanced Anatomy with Mrs. Simmons for first period."

"Ugh, blood and bones right after breakfast."

"That's right up my alley, thank you very much."

Chapter 6

After Advanced Anatomy, I headed to AP Lit. I thought the worst thing about my lit class was the teacher. Mrs. Crandall and I were far from best friends.

But as Mrs. Crandall called roll I realized the worst thing was that I shared AP Lit with Ryan *and* Noah.

When she got to Noah's name, there was no response and the class began to murmur.

"Does anyone know where Mr. James is?" she asked. "It's not like him to miss class."

"I heard he was sick," Mary Griffiths said.

"I heard he was picked up from O'Reily's by ambulance Sunday morning," Blake Courtney said.

Loud whispers spread through the class like a sound wave. I leaned across the row and whispered to Blake, "Ambulance? Seriously?"

"Yeah, I heard he was beaten up and left unconscious under a tree."

My stomach churned. I looked back at Ryan, who sat ramrod stiff with his hands in his lap. He stared over my head, refusing to make eye contact.

"Well, until I get official notification from the office, he's unexcused," Mrs. Crandall huffed. "You children must learn responsibility. You can't get through life expecting your mommas and daddies to do everything for you. Spoiled. The lot of you." She eyed me with her one good eye. "And I'll be watching you, Ariel Jane. There will be no cheating in my class this year."

I opened my mouth to respond, but felt a kick to my chair. I looked back at Ryan, and this time he didn't avoid my gaze. He gave me a warning look, and even though everything in me wanted to do the exact opposite, I bit my lip and held my tongue.

That woman made my slow-flowing blood boil. And Mom wasn't a big fan of the old rat, either. I'd thought Mom was going to come out of her skin when she got called to the counselor's office last year because

Mrs. Crandall wanted to have me suspended for cheating.

I had made an A on a test. The only A in all her classes. According to Mrs. Crandall, nobody should've scored higher than a C. Basically, I had some nerve scoring so well on the Shakespeare unit test—especially when Mrs. Crandall's idea of teaching was reading straight from the textbook.

Mom's response: "She's always been an A student. If she cheated, then prove it. If you can't, then we're done here." And she up and left, dragging me out the door with her.

Obviously, Mrs. Crandall couldn't prove it, because I never got suspended. But in her mind, I was guilty and that was all that mattered.

"Before we get started today, I've been asked by this year's senior class sponsor, Mr. Charles, to announce that the sign-up sheets for class elections are located on a table outside the main office. Please indicate by the end of today if you're planning to declare."

Mr. Charles was this year's sponsor? Awesome. I had already planned to run, but knowing that the hot man on campus was the class sponsor was extra incentive. Mr. Charles was tall and so fine that he could turn me into mush with just one wink of his big green eyes. Many a high school girl (and a few boys) have dreamed of making headlines with Mr. Charles. I wasn't one of them. Well, not really. Sure, he was fun to look at, but he was a teacher. And kinda too old for me. Total ick factor.

This was Mr. Charles's second semester at Valley Springs. He taught World History, but in his classes, you got so much more than useless dates and factoids. And I'm not just talking about his looks. Mr. Charles was an expert in occult mythology and he loved to interject bits of his specialty into all of his classes. It almost made history interesting. Almost.

Last year, during our study of the Roman Empire, we learned about a theory that vampires were descendants of Judas Iscariot. Apparently, people believed that after Judas betrayed Jesus he killed himself, and, as a punishment for his suicide, became the first vampire. Can you imagine Judas waking up and realizing he had to serve eternal damnation as a bloodsucker?

Mr. Charles also pointed out that Judas betrayed Jesus for thirty pieces of silver and perhaps that was where the myth about vampire aversion to silver originated. And maybe even their supposed aversion to crosses.

I learned something new about my people that day.

Mrs. Crandall began to pass out this year's syllabus,

droning on about how there would be no grading on a curve because we were advanced students, blah, blah, blah.

I felt Ryan before I heard him. He leaned up to my ear and his breath was an electric shock to my system. Chills spilled like a waterfall down my back, and the birthmark on my neck began to burn.

"I guess you plan on running for president again this year, especially now that Mr. 'I'm So Hot' is the sponsor," he whispered.

"Green really isn't your color, Ryan. But you do look good wearing Lindsey Rockport. Why don't you focus on wearing her out for a while and leave the other stuff to those of us who have on big-girl panties."

"Miss Ashe. We are not going to tolerate your incessant interruptions. Take your books and leave my class. I'm sure Mrs. Blanchard will be thrilled to see you already," Mrs. Crandall snapped.

"Seriously?" I asked.

"Don't take that tone with me, young lady. Go."

I stood, slung my backpack over my shoulder, and told Ryan to *eat shit and die* with my eyes. Then I reached for a syllabus.

"No, ma'am. You'll just have to do without," she said.

"Maybe you'll learn to keep your mouth shut when you come back tomorrow. *If* you get to come back tomorrow."

The intercom beeped before I left the room, and the school secretary's voice crackled through. "Mrs. Crandall, can you please send AJ Ashe to the office?"

"What a coincidence," Mrs. Crandall sneered. "She was just on her way."

Hm. Maybe my not-really-illegal parking spot just got me a really big parking ticket.

The door slammed shut behind me as I made my way down the hall toward the main office. The halls were eerily quiet since everyone was in class but me.

Honestly. Who got in trouble on the first day of the school year? I was the good girl. The overachiever. The girl who excelled at everything. I didn't smoke, didn't drink (well, wouldn't drink again), and didn't skip school. And I wasn't a ho. (The bra action with, now, two boys should not count against me.) How could one teacher hate me for the same reasons all the other teachers loved me?

Mrs. Blanchard's office was located in the main building at the front of campus. As I entered the administration area, I noticed a couple of teachers and office personnel talking quietly in a huddle, worried looks on their faces.

I knocked on the door before I entered, startling them

all. Mrs. Blanchard was in the group, along with Mrs. Grimm, the assistant principal. Both the girls' and boys' soccer coaches were there. Coach Landers looked like his world had just split in two.

"We're not quite ready for you, AJ," Mrs. Grimm, the assistant principal, said. "Please wait outside."

What was going on?

There were two chairs set up outside the office, along with the registration table for class officer. I wandered over to the table to put my name in the running. A dozen other kids—all girls—had already signed up to run for several of the offices. Nobody had signed up for president yet.

As I was writing my name under the president column, I concentrated on the hushed voices mumbling on the other side of the wall. I might not have complete control over my vampire abilities, but one thing I had learned very early on was how to hone in on my hearing. Admittedly, I mostly used my extra-sharp hearing for gossip gathering, but every once in a while it came in handy for other purposes. Like eavesdropping in the office to see how much trouble I was in.

I focused on my ears, and my senses opened as the soft hum of voices turned to conversation.

"This is going to be a huge blow to the student body.

We have to call an assembly," Mrs. Blanchard said.

"I agree, but I need to tell my kids first. The soccer team is going to be devastated," Coach Landers croaked.

"What about additional counselors?" Miss Mandy, the office manager, asked.

"The hospital contacted a group for us. They'll be here after lunch. We'll announce the assembly for one o'clock. Coach Landers, we'll also make an announcement for the soccer team to report to the gym immediately so you can prepare them. Now, who wants to break the news?"

"I will," Mrs. Grimm said. "It needs to come from either myself or the principal. And since Mr. Ward is with the family, I think I should be the one." Her voice broke. "I can't believe Noah James is dead."

Chapter 7

oah was dead?

My hands went cold and my heart stuttered from slow to stop.

Was I the last person to see Noah alive? Is that why they had called me to the office?

The office door opened, and Mrs. Blanchard motioned me inside.

"Your mother called. You need to pick up your sisters from school today," she said, handing me the message. She looked at me, "AJ, are you okay?"

I nodded. "Um, yeah. Mrs. Crandall told me to come see you because she said I was disrupting class."

"Well, this isn't a good time for that. Here, take this to

Mrs. Crandall and tell her to get over it," she said, scribbling a note onto a piece of paper. "Actually, strike that last comment. Please don't tell her to get over it, otherwise you'll both wind up back here."

"Yes, ma'am," I said, my voice cracking.

"And one more thing," she said, handing me the note. "You park illegally again, you're going to have detention for a week, okay?"

I nodded and turned to leave, but she grabbed my hand, stopping me. "You're as pale as a ghost, AJ."

My throat burned, and no matter how hard I swallowed, I couldn't dislodge the lump of fear.

"How did he die?" I asked.

"Oh, honey. I'm so sorry you found out like this. Sit down," she said, guiding me to Miss Mandy's office chair. "He was found in a coma yesterday morning at O'Reily's farm. They're not sure what killed him. He was pretty beaten up, it seems. But then, it also appears he was bitten by a snake. We'll know more after the autopsy."

"Bitten?" I sobbed. Tears burned my lids as a picture of my spattered tank and the blood on my pillow flashed through my mind.

Oh my God. What had I done?

"Miss Mandy, get AJ some water," Mrs. Blanchard

said, never letting go of my hand. "AJ, do I need to call your mom?"

"No, ma'am," I whispered. More tears spilled down my face, and suddenly I was very cold. "A snakebite? Where?"

"On his wrist."

I gasped. The vampire neck fetish was mostly glamorized by Hollywood. Sure, if there was a neck available at the time, vamps would go for it. But if they wanted to disguise the bite, they often went for the ankle.

Or the wrist.

"I've gotta go," I said as Miss Mandy handed me a Dixie cup full of water. I shook my head and pushed her hand away. "I'm sorry, but I really have to get out of here."

I rushed out of the office in a flurry, nearly knocking Malia over as she entered.

"Hey! Watch out," she yelled.

"Sorry," I mumbled, not even looking back.

I had to get out of there. I ran to my car at full speed, jumped in, and started it up. As I backed out of the parking lot, I pulled my phone out and dialed the hospital.

My mom's secretary answered.

"Laura, this is AJ. Is Mom around?"

"She's in a patient consult right now, AJ."

"I'm gonna be there in ten minutes. Please tell her it's an emergency. I need her."

"Okay, darling. Can I do anything for you?"

"Just get my mom," I said, snapping my phone closed.

My birthmark burned and my head ached as all sorts of things ran through my mind. I still didn't remember getting home after the bonfire. I just remember being pissed off at Noah for forcing me to touch him.

I *had* been drinking . . . was it possible that I was so angry, I went back after Noah? I watch TV—people black out and kill all the time. I just never thought that *I* was capable of blacking out and biting.

Sacred Heart Hospital loomed two blocks away. It's ironic that most hospitals are religiously sponsored and that many doctors are vampires. Vampires really are totally misunderstood by the religious world. Sure, thousands of years ago we were evil, but now? Not so much. Okay, we have a few bad eggs left in our bunch, but overall, we're just souped-up humans.

Kinda like superheroes. With fangs. And, um, a slight penchant for blood.

Was I one of the bad eggs? I had always assumed the bad guys *know* they were evil. You know, they were just born that way. But maybe that isn't the case. Maybe the bad guys just have no control over their instincts. Maybe they black out every time they do something evil. Is that what happened to me?

If so, my next confession could prove to be interesting. Maybe I should've gone to Mass yesterday instead of the mall. How many Hail Marys would it take to erase the sin of sucking the life out of someone?

I pulled into the parking deck and found a spot on the first level. My head continued to throb as I shot through the lobby to the elevator. I punched level four and waited.

And waited.

The doors finally closed and the elevator began to creep upward. I probably could've walked up the stairs faster than taking the elevators. I always forget how slow these stupid things are.

Finally, the box lurched to a stop and the doors opened. I stepped into the hallway, turned right, and headed toward Mom's office.

She was waiting for me at Laura's desk. "Are you okay?" she asked as I rushed in.

"Yeah. No. I don't know."

Mom wrapped her arms around me and led me into her office. "Laura, hold my calls and reschedule all my morning appointments."

The plump brunette nodded. "I hope everything's okay, AJ. If I can do anything, just holler. Oh, and AJ? The kids were asking about you the other day. You're their favorite babysitter," she said.

I turned and smiled at Laura as Mom closed the door behind us. I walked to the oversized leather sofa and collapsed into a ball of tears as panic snaked through my body.

"AJ, you're starting to scare me. What's this about?" Mom sat beside me and I buried my head into her lab coat, staining it with my runny mascara.

"Momma, I think I've done something terrible. I mean, I think I *could've* done something terrible," I heaved.

She reached over to the side table and picked up the box of tissues. "Sit up, blow your nose, and start from the beginning. I can't help you if you keep speaking in riddles."

Dread threaded its way up my spine as I tried to figure out how to break my mom's heart. I mean, what mother could love pure evil? I've seen *The Omen*. I know.

Of course, it wasn't my fault if I hadn't evolved like the rest of my race. Maybe my genetic strands were just stunted. Great. I was a Cro-Magnon vampire. As if being evil wasn't bad enough, now I had underdeveloped evolutionary growth. Wonder if there's a nunnery for evil Cro-Magnon vampire girls?

I sighed, wiped my puffy eyes, and broke the news to Mom. "I think I'm evil."

Mom's eyes went wide, then her laughter bubbled around me like carbonation. "Honey, what are you talking about? You don't have an evil bone in your body."

"I think I killed Noah James. I don't remember it, but I think I did it. I mean, I must've done it. I was so mad at him. He tried to force me to touch him and he called me a tease, then I blacked out and then I woke up with blood everywhere and he was dead."

Mom's laughter fell flat. "The snakebite victim? That was the boy you made out with at O'Reily's?" she asked.

I nodded. "You heard about him?"

"I was called in for a consult before he died. The venom was stopping his heart and we were looking at surgical options. But he'd lost a lot of blood from internal bleeding. There was nothing we could do."

"Internal bleeding from a bite? Isn't that unusual?" I asked.

"He had bruising on his chest and abdomen. They think the battering is actually what put him in the coma.

When he was bitten, chances are he wasn't awake."

"Oh," I gasped, remembering the rage on Ryan's face as he stayed behind to chat with Noah.

"There is no way you could've inflicted that kind of damage to him. You aren't big enough or strong enough, and you haven't exhibited any superhuman strength, have you?"

I shook my head.

"So there's no way you could've been involved."

"But a boy could have?"

"Maybe, if he used a crowbar. The bruising was pretty excessive."

"What about the snakebite? What if I'm venomous?"

"Well, that is something we definitely need to find out. Because, I'm sorry to say, that could very well be true."

"What are you saying, Mom?"

She looked at me.

"I'm saying your father is full-blooded Serpentine, so it's possible you inherited the venomous bite. I'll need to run some tests—and I guess it's time you learn about some dark family history."

I'm a descendant of the Serpentine Clan? I reached up and touched my birthmark, then did a mental head slap.

Well, duh. Of course I am. I knew the Serpentines had the S-shaped mark—it just never dawned on me that my backward S was their mark as well. I guess I've been swimming in the River Denial my whole life.

"Make your fangs descend," Mom ordered.

"I can't." Okay, I could. It just took some concentration. But I didn't want to.

"AJ, just do it. Not knowing doesn't do you any good. I can test your venom against the venom in Noah's body. We have to know if it's the same."

"What if I'm evil?" I asked.

On an evil scale from one to ten, the Serpentines rated a twelve. They're the vamps you hear about—the ones who kill simply for the thrill of it. They're also race purists who believe they're the only vampires worthy of life, and they rule their clan with an iron fist. No Serpentine is allowed to breed outside of the race—if they do, they're immediately excommunicated. And in some cases, executed. Some family, huh?

And I was a descendant. Another moment of irony as I realized I had not only fallen for someone outside my clan, but someone outside the vampire race completely. Methinks the clan elders definitely would not approve.

"You're not evil; now pop out those fangs for me."

So, you know how on Animal Planet that crazy snake dude "milks" the venom from whatever rare and endangered serpent he just caught in some remote jungle off the coast of wherever? Well, my mom milked me.

That's just not right.

"There," she said, sealing the syrupy clear liquid up in the tube. "It will probably take a few days to run the tests, but until then, I don't want you to worry. I *know* you didn't do this, AJ."

"I wish I could be as sure about that as you are."

She smiled. "Hang on just a second," she said, walking over to her desk. She clicked the intercom button on her phone. "Laura?"

"Yes?"

"My rounds today are at three, is that correct?"

"Yes, ma'am."

"Okay, thanks." She disconnected and then dialed another extension. "Octavia?" she asked. "Can you come to my office for a minute?" She paused to listen. "Yes, bring it with you. See you in a second."

"Was that Auntie Tave?" I asked when she hung up. "I haven't seen her since you finished your internship. I was surprised she wasn't at the wedding."

"She was on her way home from a blood bank inspection

on Saturday. We're actually pretty lucky to have caught her, since she travels so much. You know, I couldn't have survived your father leaving without Octavia. And if you want proof that you didn't bite Noah, Auntie Tave is just the person who can give it to you. She's on her way."

Chapter 8

"Why didn't you tell us that we were Serpentines?" I asked while we waited.

Growing up, I'd done my best to disregard my vampire side, but there are some parts of our past that can't be ignored. Overall, vampires are well educated in the ways of the reportedly "evil" clans. It's no different from being taught about the Nazis or Jim Jones, I guess. It's just an ugly part of our history and we're taught about it in the hope that we won't make the same mistakes.

You've got the Serpentines with their deadly venom and their superiority complex. The Shifters and their ability to shapeshift into other beings. And then there were the old-timers, the vampires who were created by being bitten, direct descendants of Judas, if you believe that theory. Infected humans, so to speak. They're few and far between now, but their history is so gruesome that humans believe all vampire-kind are the same. Blood-thirsty, unfeeling killing machines.

Genetic vampires refer to the old-timers as dichampyrs nowadays, because they struggle with their dichotomy. It's not easy being half-human and half-vampire. (Okay, technically, I'm part-human and part-vampire, but it's different because I was born this way. My human DNA doesn't treat the vampire DNA like it's an infection—theirs does.)

Oh, and genetic vampires aren't immortal, either. We have beating hearts. As long as a vamp feeds, its heart works. I suppose we *could* live forever, but like with any living thing, when you stop the heart, you die. It's the one organ that doesn't seem to heal. Don't ask me why. Google really ought to come up with a special vampire search engine.

And it doesn't matter what you drive through the heart. Wooden stakes work, but they're not required. Hollywood sure likes them, though. I guess there'd be no onscreen conflict if Buffy could've used anything within reach to dust a vamp.

There are dichamps who allow the infection to take

over and they completely stamp down their human side. But it's the ones who can't let go of their human side who have the hardest time with the change. They can't feel, they can't breathe, they can't taste, and they only find joy in consuming blood. They lose their connection to the little things that made life worth living. But they still remember those things, which makes it damn miserable for them to exist. They're the ones who go crazy. Eventually, they stop feeding. It's like vampire depression.

Wonder if GlaxoSmithKline makes a pill for that?

Genetically born vampires' human and vampire sides are fused together. We're just as much human as we are vampire.

And frankly, I consider myself to be *way* more human than vampire. . . .

"Your father and I wanted to protect you," Mom said, interrupting my train of thought.

I couldn't help but laugh. I hadn't seen my dad since I was in single digits, and the thought of him wanting to do anything but abandon me was funny as hell.

"Dad sure stuck around for the whole 'protection plan' thing, didn't he?"

Mom's eyes got a little cloudy. "I loved your father, but he wasn't ready for the hand we were dealt."

"You weren't, either, Mom, but somehow you managed to be great at it."

She smiled. "Some people grow up faster than others. Your father was passionate and rebellious. And we fell hard for each other. Of course, we were forbidden to see each other. I wasn't full-blooded Serpentine. Even though I had the mark," she said, lifting her pant leg to expose the S-shaped mark on her calf.

I touched my neck. It had never dawned on me that my birthmark was more than just something I'd inherited from my mother. Clearly, denial was my new BFF.

Mom continued. "I had too much human in me, therefore I was 'unclean.' The clan elders had already arranged your father's future marriage. But your dad loved me. We kept seeing each other. And then I got pregnant. . . ." Her voice trailed off slightly before she added, "And I don't regret that one bit. I'll never regret my children."

I smiled and laid my head on her shoulder. "That's a given, Mom."

"Your father was so happy about you. We ran away and got married. The clan came after your father, but he stood by us. He told them to take a hike. They kept coming back, kept mentioning some prophecy, but your father just pooh-poohed it and ignored them. I never understood exactly what they were talking about, but this prophecy was directly responsible for their views on breeding outside the clan.

"We moved to a college town, where we both got our degrees, and then I started med school. The clan seemed to finally give up on your father and left us alone. Then, not long after you turned nine, your dad just up and left. I never really understood what happened exactly. He sent me divorce papers and I heard he eventually married the woman the elders had handpicked for him before."

"Dad remarried?"

"Yes. You know, I really can't blame your father. He did try. But we were both young, and stupid to believe we could defy the clan."

Mom's intercom buzzed. "Octavia is here, Liz," Laura said.

Mom stood and walked to the door. "Are you ready for this?" she asked as Auntie Tave rushed inside.

"Lizzie! I'm so glad you called, but you know you didn't have to. I was about to head this way when my phone buzzed." She turned to me and her elfin smile doubled in size. "And AJ, I haven't seen you in forever! Come here and give Auntie Tave a hug."

Octavia wrapped me into a bear hug. She was surprisingly strong for such a petite little thing. I couldn't gauge her age, but she was probably somewhere in her sixties. Not that she looked it.

Her hair was cropped super short and it was flaming orange. She had a splotch of gray at her right temple. She wore lipstick that matched her hair and she had the grayest eyes I had ever seen.

When I hugged her back my head was suddenly filled with memories of drawing on the driveway with chalk, eating red licorice ropes.

"What happened to your blue-tipped black hair?" I asked with a laugh.

"Oh, that was ages ago." She laughed. "I've matured since then," she said with a wink.

She sat in the chair across from me and answered the question I hadn't asked. "So you didn't know I worked here? Well, I do—when I'm not doing quality checks at the other facilities, that is. I'm the blood bank goddess around these parts. How much do you know about hemoshake production?" she asked me.

"Um. I know they're packaged like V8s or tomato soup. That's about it."

"I suppose that's all you really need to know, huh? Well, if you ever want a tour of the hemoshake plant, let me know," she said. "It's located beneath the hospital and I can get you the VIP tour."

"Okay," I said. "I had no idea the plant was here. That's kinda cool."

Octavia leaned over and patted my knee. "You also have no idea why I'm here, do you?"

"No, ma'am," I answered truthfully.

"I'm here because your momma knows I can tell if you've bitten someone. I have a gift."

Hope blossomed in my chest. "Awesome! Because I *really* need to know what happened."

"I know you're worried; I felt it all the way in my office when you stepped into the hospital."

She reached into her bag and pulled out a box. "Let's get this going. I'm going to do two things with you, okay? The first thing I'm going to ask for is a venom sample."

"Seriously? But I just gave one to Mom." I looked over at Momma.

"How much do you need, Tave? I've got a vial, but I'm still planning to run a test against the venom in the boy."

"Just a couple of drops." Octavia opened the box and

pulled out a stick that looked amazingly like a pregnancy test.

"Do I have to pee on that?"

Octavia's laugh was deep and full of warmth. "No, honey. I'm working with the Vampire Commission to get a patent for this little test. If you bit Noah, there will be some of his DNA residue in your venom. But this test is only about seventy-five percent accurate, so I have to continue to develop it until I get much more precise results. I think we're going to call it Clearbite Easy. Clever, huh?"

"Uh, sure. The Vampire Commission?"

Tave stared at Mom.

"Lizzie, have you not told this child anything about our world? Shame on you."

My mom just laughed as she handed Octavia the vial. "Don't blame me. This *child* is much happier pretending that vampires are just a myth. I've given her the history, and I promise to tell her more in the future. It was just easier to let her pretend, until now. It felt safer that way. You know, with Clive going back to the Serpentines and all."

Tave waved her hand dismissively. "Your husband was weak. Good thing you had me to get you through. Now,

AJ, I need you to close your eyes and hold out your hands, palms up. I'm assuming your mother has taught you how to focus on the white? I need you to do that for me now. And I have to warn you, whatever you start seeing I'll see as well. Are you ready?"

"I guess so."

I did exactly as she instructed. Octavia held my hands in hers, and I focused on the white.

It took a few minutes to get the canvas behind my eyes to go blank. I'm sure some part of me was resisting. Part of me didn't want to know if I had bitten Noah. A very strong part of me.

But finally the white appeared, and I relaxed a bit. My palms grew warm. The heat spread from my hands, up my arms, into my body.

The white sparked bright, and suddenly it was Saturday night again. I was watching myself with Noah. I saw his anger when I stopped things. The more I watched, the more alive my own anger grew.

My mind flashed forward. But the only thing I could see was darkness. I felt only fury. Fierce anger like nothing I'd ever experienced before.

Suddenly, I was no longer standing in the dark; I was running through the woods—crying. My shirt was soaked with blood and I was hysterical. Where was everyone? What had happened?

Octavia released my hands, startled.

"AJ, AJ!" she said.

She and my mom were both calling to me, but I couldn't seem to come back to them. I couldn't find them.

I heard a smack and my face stung. "AJ, dammit! Wake up," Mom yelled.

The connection was finally broken, and I collapsed back in the chair, exhausted. I looked at Octavia's face, and a sense of dread bloomed inside me.

"Did I bite Noah?"

"Honey, something definitely happened, but I have no idea what. I couldn't tell if that was a real memory or a dream. This has never happened before," she said. "I saw you running, I felt your panic, but your thoughts were blank. Empty. There was nothing but fear and anger. And blood."

She picked up the Clearbite Easy test and said, "The good news is, the test is negative."

"Yeah, but with only a seventy-five percent accuracy," I said. "And I did slice his tongue, so shouldn't it read positive?"

"The DNA transfer happens when you actively inject

someone with your venom. An incidental slice to the tongue wouldn't do it," Tave assured me.

My mom looked at me. "If Octavia's test says you didn't bite Noah, then I believe it."

I wished I could be so sure.

ctavia had left and I was finishing off a hemoshake trying to recover when the intercom buzzed.

"Excuse me, Liz, I'm sorry to interrupt, but there's a police officer here asking to see AJ."

"Just a moment, Laura," Mom said. She walked around the desk and held my hand tightly. "You don't have to speak to him yet if you're not ready."

"Why would he want to speak to me?"

"I'm sure they're interviewing all the kids at the party. Like I said, if you're not ready—"

"No. I'm fine. Just don't leave me."

Mom opened her office door and invited the officer

inside. My nervousness zipped out of me when I saw Cody Littleton. Thank God it wasn't the big dog, Sheriff Al Christopher. Cody is just a couple of years older than me, so he is a puppy compared to Big Al.

"Thank you, ma'am," Cody said, removing his tan deputy hat as he entered the room. His reddish brown hair is cut military short, which would be intimidating if it weren't counterbalanced by his freckled face and soft green eyes.

"Hiya, AJ," he said with a nod.

"Hey, Cody."

He walked over to the couch and sat next to me, placing his hat on his lap. He played with the rim like he was nervous. "I'm real sorry about your friend. And I'm even sorrier that I have to ask you some questions."

"It's all right."

He pulled out his spiral notebook and flipped through a couple of pages. "Several people reported that they saw you and Noah together on Saturday night. Is that true?"

I glanced over at Mom, and she reassured me with a smile. "Yes," I answered.

"How together were you?"

"What do you mean, Cody?" my mother snapped.

He glanced nervously from his notebook to me to my

mother. "I'm sorry, Dr.—"

"It's Fraser now," Mom said, when he hesitated at her last name.

"Dr. Fraser. I do apologize for having to ask such an indelicate question. But we have reports that AJ and Noah were quite close on Saturday night, if you get my drift."

My cheeks burned red—almost as red as Cody's. Maybe having Mom stay for my questioning wasn't such a brilliant idea. Nothing quite like being questioned about your sex life in front of your mom by the southern version of Ron Weasley.

"I get your drift just fine, young man. What does that have to do with his death?"

"Well, ma'am. It seems your stepson was seen with Noah, too." He cleared his throat. "He apparently caught AJ and Noah in a compromising position. We have reports that Ryan was jealous and angry. And since he was the last person seen with Noah and since it looks like Noah had been in a fight before he died . . ." He trailed off to let us draw our own conclusions.

"That's not what happened," I blurted out before I could stop myself. I mean, it was kinda what happened, but not exactly. And I knew Ryan had nothing to do with Noah's death. "There was no way Ryan beat Noah up and just left him there. He's not that guy."

"Oh? Well, by all means, clear this up for us, AJ. All we want is a firsthand account of the situation."

"Noah and I did go off into the woods together and we did make out for a little bit. But then I stopped things because it was getting out of hand and I wasn't ready."

"And he was okay with you stopping?"

"No. He tried to force me to touch him and when he stuck his tongue down my throat again, I bit it."

"And is that when Ryan found you?"

"Yes, but not just Ryan. Bridget Craig and Malia Gervase were with him."

"What happened then?" he asked, steadily making notes on the pad.

"I told Noah off, and we left."

"All of you?"

This wasn't fair. I had to tell the truth, even though my gut told me Ryan hadn't done anything. If anyone was to blame, it was me. I couldn't lie to a police officer, could I? No. Never. I couldn't.

Not even for Ryan.

"Yes, we all left together."

Never mind, I guess I could. Great. Looks like I just purchased a one-way ticket on the handbasket to hell.

Cody cocked a copper eyebrow. "You and the girls, right?"

"No, all of us. Ryan, too."

"Hm," Cody said, scribbling another note. I leaned over to try to see what he was writing, but he closed the notebook before I could get a good look.

"Hm, what?" I asked.

"Nothing for you to worry about, AJ. Thank you for your time. We'll be back in touch if we have any more questions."

Cody placed his hat back on his head and tipped it toward Mom. "Thank ya kindly, Dr. Fraser."

"You're welcome, Cody. Give my best to your momma."

Mom closed the door, then turned back toward me with her arms folded across her chest. "What's gotten into you?" she accused. "First you booze it up at a party and now you're lying to a police officer. This is just not like you, AJ."

"What?" I said, trying not to stammer. "What do you mean?"

"I saw that look on your face just before you answered that last question. You *lied* to him."

I sighed. "Mom, do you think Ryan beat Noah up?"

"No. But—"

"But nothing. He didn't. I know it, and you know it."

"You lied to keep him out of trouble. That is never a smart thing to do. You need to call Cody right now and tell him the truth."

"I already told you, we all left together."

"Ariel Jane, this will come back to bite you in the ass, and you know it."

"Well, it's something I'll have to live with, then. Ryan couldn't do that to Noah. He couldn't do that to anyone."

"AJ, you're not a liar. You've never been a liar. Why do this?"

My heart felt like a wrung-out washcloth. She was right. The truth had always been important to me, even though I live a lie every day. Now that I think about it, honesty is important *because* I live this lie. It's not easy being one thing and pretending to be something else.

Lying didn't feel right. But I could live with it, because Ryan getting into trouble over something I know he didn't do would've felt much, much worse.

"Ryan wasn't there. We *all* left together."

With those four words I completed my transformation from Dudette Do-Right to Little Miss Deviant.

○○○

Guilt clung to me like Saran Wrap as I drove home. The more I tried to shake my brain clear, the more layers of cling wrap I had to fight. My gut knotted and my heart hammered as I worked to force any thought of Noah out of my brain.

But I couldn't get rid of him. The more I struggled, the more I felt suffocated by my own apprehension.

I pulled into the driveway to find Ryan waiting for me.

"We need to talk," he said as I closed the car door.

"Can't this wait?"

"I don't think so. C'mon." He grabbed me by the elbow and escorted me to the backyard. A tire swing swayed gently in the breeze, practically inviting me to sit down. So I did.

"I'm tired, Ryan. I really don't have anything to say."

"Are you okay?" he asked, his brown eyes dark with worry.

"Never better." I laughed bitterly and toed the ground, launching the tire into a creaky sway.

"Cody Littleton came to see me today," Ryan said. "He thinks I beat Noah up and left him unconscious."

"Yeah, I got that feeling. He came to see me, too."

"I *wanted* to kill Noah, but I didn't."

"I know that. You don't have it in you to hurt someone

like that. If you were that guy, I wouldn't have ever gone out with you in the first place." Much less let him under my shirt.

"I'm really sorry about Saturday night." He paused. "I miss you."

I missed him, too. I looked into his dark eyes and sighed as a blanket of chills covered me. It would be so easy to forget today. To forget Noah and the possibility that I was evil in a short skirt and just run away with Ryan like my parents had done. Of course, we all know what a good idea that had been.

"Ryan, I—"

Ryan stopped the swing and pulled me into a hug. I breathed in his scent. Earthy, spicy, and magically delicious. He pulled back, took my face in his hands. I closed my eyes and brought my hands to his arms, waiting for a kiss that shouldn't happen, but one I needed with every drop of blood in my body.

He leaned in and I mirrored the motion, sliding my palm along his arm to his hand. I felt him flinch and it startled me. I opened my eyes and pulled his right hand off my face and glanced at his knuckles.

My heart fell when I saw the bruises and swelling. Grabbing his left hand, I removed the Band-Aids that covered his swollen knuckles. Dried blood crusted around the open wounds.

"You lied to me." The irony of the situation hit me in the gut like an iron mallet.

"No."

"Yes. You did. And I covered for you." My hands were shaking. My voice cracked.

"I never asked you to do that, AJ."

"I told Cody you left with me last night."

"Why would you do something so stupid? Now it just makes me look guilty!"

"Isn't that what you are?" My insides were a jumble of live wires sparking and shocking their way through my system. Had I been wrong about Ryan? Did he beat Noah up and leave him there for me to suck the remaining breath from his unconscious body? Were we like some anti-superhero duo, working together to spread our evil stepsibling karma across the planet?

"I covered for you! I lied for you! I hate liars and now you've turned me into one."

"I never asked you to cover for me, AJ. Don't blame your stupidity on me. Living a lie can be a bitch, so either come clean or deal with it."

Who the hell was he talking to about living a lie? I

was the queen of dichotomy. Perfect little human girl on the outside. Raging out-of-control vamp on the inside. I knew lies. I just didn't like liars. (Yes, I know. I'm also a hypocrite.)

"Oh, that's rich coming from you. I hope you're ready to take your own advice. So you want me to call Cody and tell him, or are you going to, as you put it, 'come clean or deal with it'?"

"I didn't kill Noah," he said quietly.

"Are you sure?" I asked.

His silence was all the answer I needed. "The water can get really cold in the River Denial," I said.

And I should know.

Chapter 10

What else could go wrong?

(Okay, just for the record, one should never ask that question, 'cause inevitably something else will happen. . . .)

It really wasn't like Ryan to keep things from me—especially important things like "Oh, by the way, I beat the shit outta Noah last night but I didn't kill him. He was alive and kicking when I left."

The truth was, I no more believed Ryan killed Noah than I believed in Santa Claus. The bigger truth—no matter what my momma and that "bite" test said, I still had doubts about my own innocence. I could only hope I'd feel better when Momma got those venom test results back.

The guilt weighed like a wet blanket, heavy on my back and shoulders, as I thought about Noah. Suddenly I could smell moss and wet leaves. As I had been in my mom's office, I was transported back to Saturday night, to the moment I licked the sweat from his neck. My heart kicked it up a notch and my mouth watered.

But a movement by the window startled me. I shifted to glance outside as the hairs on my neck stood on end. I quickly scanned the woods.

I was going out of my mind. As if someone was really out there watching me. From my second-floor window. What a schizo.

My cell phone rang as I crossed myself and pulled the shade down. My Catholic guilt might make me paranoid, but it didn't hurt to cover my window, anyway.

I sat down on the edge of my bed and answered, "Hello." Spike stretched and meandered over to me, plopping down on my lap.

"Hey," Malia said. "Are you okay? You nearly plowed me over running out of the office today."

"Yeah. I'm fine. I had just found out about Noah and was totally out of my head. Sorry about that."

"No prob. Finding out about Noah nearly did everyone in. They released us after the announcement today.

You could've heard a pin drop in the gym when they told us. Except for the sniffling, it was dead quiet."

Dead quiet. How appropriate.

"So, anyway, I was calling to warn you about tomorrow," Malia said with an edge to her voice.

"Tomorrow?"

"Yeah. Can you believe Crabby Crandall scheduled a pop quiz for tomorrow? She's giving us a ten-question test over tonight's reading assignment. That woman is completely out of her mind! She knows everyone is in shock over Noah and that the reading won't get done. Oh, and I heard they're having a memorial service tomorrow. You wanna go after school?"

I sighed and felt my shoulders slump. The very idea of going to Noah's memorial service made me sick to my stomach. "Yeah. Let's go together. I'm sure Bridget will come, too. So, how did you find out about the test? Is it on the syllabus?" The one I didn't get.

"I don't think so. I was still registering during her class, so I didn't get a syllabus. I overheard her talking to her evil minion assistant outside of the teachers' lounge after all the students were dismissed today. They were both so giddy, their dried-up raisin faces were almost plump with delight."

"Dammit. I don't wanna study tonight. But I also don't wanna fail her test. I don't think I could handle that condescending smirk of hers right now. I guess I don't have a choice."

"This is crap, AJ. Don't do the reading. She can't do anything if everyone fails."

"If you didn't want me to study, you shouldn't have told me about the quiz."

"Whatever. Mrs. Crandall shouldn't be such a hard-shell crab."

Yeah, but failing her test wouldn't soften that shell anytime soon. As a matter of fact, I've always suspected Mrs. Crandall is a little bit (okay, a lot bit) of a sadist who takes pleasure in failing kids and making us miserable. So if there *is* a mass failing tomorrow, Mrs. Crandall might feel like she's in heaven.

I walked over to the mini-fridge next to my bed and pulled out a hemoshake. Exhaustion settled in. My eyes were heavy and my brain was this side of mush. I caved to the realization that there would be no studying tonight. So I flipped on the television and zoned out to some *Buffy the Vampire Slayer* reruns.

Maybe Angel and Spike would send me into a pleasant night of sexy vampire dreams.

Scritch, scritch, scritch.

It was dark. My eyelids were so heavy, I couldn't open them, but my heart was racing. Something had woken me from my death-sleep.

Scritch, scritch, scritch.

There it was again. My heart pounded loudly in my ears as I heard the scratching on my window. Like an insistent pet, scratching at the door to come back inside.

But my cat was curled up next to me, and I was on the second floor, anyway.

Scritch, scritch, scritch.

Maybe it was a breeze blowing a branch against the window.

I focused my hearing to listen for the wind. But I heard nothing.

I jumped up and flung the shades open. Nothing to see, either.

With my heart hammering in my head, I climbed back in bed and waited for the sunrise.

I wish I could say I was bright-eyed and bushy-tailed when the sun finally rose, but that definitely was not the case. After jumping out of bed, I hadn't managed even one ounce of sleep. Whenever I did get my eyes to close, the hairs on my neck would stand straight up, and I'd hear the scratching on my window or a whispering in the distance. I'd check; nothing would be outside.

Still, I was totally creeped out. So to shake myself awake, I decided to pound my fatigue into the ground with a long run.

I threw myself into my running gear. I walked through the kitchen to leave a note for the family and, instead, found a note waiting for me.

Ariel dear,
This necklace is made from red Jasper, mined in Scotland. I hope you like it. I have given your sisters bracelets made from the same stone. I'm so glad you're a part of our family.
Aunt Doreen

How sweet. The necklace was a simple gold chain with two interlocking triangles carved in the multi-shaded red stone. I clipped it around my neck and hit the road.

The sun had barely winked at me over the horizon,

but the air already felt heavy and thick like wet cotton. It was definitely going to be "Mississippi hot" today.

Sweat ran down my face as I sprinted the last block toward home. Even in the light of day I couldn't shake the feeling that I was being watched. I stopped a few times and looked around but saw only the occasional animal or bird.

The feeling never went away.

With each step, my lungs felt heavier, my heart stuttered, and the hairs on my neck stayed at attention. Obviously, the fatigue and guilt were getting to me. Five miles felt like five hundred, but on the bright side, I was too tired to worry about anything but a shower right then.

The house was still quiet, as the rest of the brood wouldn't start rising for another half hour or so. Hopefully Ryan would make a quick exit like he did yesterday. I really wasn't in the mood to face him.

"Good mornin' to ye, dearie," Aunt Doreen said from behind me. I swear, that woman just appeared out of thin air. "Would ye care for some tea?" she asked.

"No, thank you. I'm just gonna go take a quick shower."

"I see ye picked up your trinket," she said.

"I did! Thank you so much. I love it!"

She smiled and touched my shoulder. "That symbol is

the Seal of Solomon and it's verra special, just like you. Ye seem a bit fashed. What's troublin' ye, wee one?"

Wee one. That was funny coming from a woman who stood a good six inches shorter than me.

"I'm just tired from my run."

"Ah, so this running you did, it gives you worry lines around the eyes, then? Doesna seem like somethin' I'd do willingly if it made me look old before my time."

"No. The running helps the worry lines. I actually feel better now."

"Oh, dear me. That sounds dreadful. You must've looked a fright before. Doesna seem fair, aye? Such large worries being put on such young shoulders."

"I've heard people say life's not fair more times than I can count."

"There's no' a truth greater than that one. However, if life were fair, it'd be a smidge more boring, I think."

"Yes, ma'am."

I smiled and turned toward the stairs.

"Ariel, dear?"

"Yes?"

"Fate is a funny creature. She puts obstacles in your path to see what kind of character ye have. Life isn't fair, life is a test."

"Aunt Doreen, if that's true, then I'm in a heap of trouble because I haven't studied one lick."

Malia and Bridget were waiting for me at my locker between first and second period.

"So, did you study for Crandall's torture session this morning?" Malia asked.

"No, but I had plenty of time, so I should have. I didn't sleep a wink."

"You do look like shit, even if your outfit is kickin'," Bridget said, giving me the once-over.

"You're the second person today to tell me that. I must really look bad."

"Just tired," Malia interjected, shooting Bridget a look. "Which is understandable, given the circumstances."

Bridget raised her eyebrows and tightened her lips.

"It's not every day you get to be the last person someone will ever kiss," I muttered.

"That makes it sound romantic. It wasn't romantic. I'm sorry he died, but he shouldn't have done that to you, AJ. He was a prick and though he didn't deserve to die, he surely didn't deserve you, either." Bridget's hackles were up and she was in full-fledged-friend mode.

"Thanks, Bridge," I said as the bell rang. "I guess it's time to face the music that is Crabby Crandall. Hey, are you going to Noah's memorial service today?"

"You haven't heard?" Bridget asked.

"Heard what?" I asked.

"Noah's body is missing. They can't find it anywhere. My mom thinks he was accidentally cremated and the funeral home doesn't want to admit it. Apparently this funeral home has a history of mixing people up," Bridget said.

"Accidentally cremated? Really?"

"Well, what other explanation would there be? That Noah just got up and walked out on his own?"

Fear tickled my spine.

What if he hadn't been misplaced or accidentally cremated?

What if he *had* walked out on his own—?

Oh, God.

I needed to puke.

"Hey, we've gotta go," Malia said. "I finally got my schedule this morning. It looks like I'm in three of your classes, starting with Mrs. Crandall's. Are you okay? You look a little pale."

"I'm fine," I said, shaking the fear from my head. "Let's face Crabby Crandall together, then. See ya, Bridge."

As we walked toward class, a couple of jocks ran past us, nearly knocking us over. They missed us, but not Meredith Taylor. She was just turning away from her locker when they bumped into her, sending her books and papers flying.

"Watch it, meatheads!" I yelled, rushing to Meredith's aid as everyone else in the hall just laughed. "We're not required to wear helmets in the hall, but maybe we should be. Here, let me help."

I gathered her papers as she picked up her books. "Thanks," she said. "You didn't have to—"

"Sure I did," I replied with a smile.

She smiled back.

Meredith hesitated. After a few awkward seconds she finally spoke. "You know, for the record, I think it really sucks that you and Ryan had to split up because of your parents."

"It does suck, but I'll get over it. I don't have a choice."

"Lindsey's my best friend, and I'm happy she's finally with the boy she wanted, but I'm worried. I really like Ryan, but I'm just afraid she's going to wind up getting hurt. Nobody wants to be the rebound girl."

"I can tell you from experience that good friends ease

the pain of a broken heart." I laughed. "Okay, not really. But they make me laugh and that does help. All you can do is be there for her if she needs you."

"I can do that," she said.

"Even though we're not on each other's pom-squad, I really hope Lindsey doesn't get hurt. Getting over Ryan Fraser isn't very easy. And that's a fact."

Meredith smiled sympathetically. "Thanks again, AJ."

When Malia and I walked into the classroom, the busy hum of chatter came to an abrupt and very noticeable halt. I guess everyone knew I was the last person to see Noah alive. Great. AJ Ashe—kiss of death? Talk amongst yourselves. I took my seat in front of Ryan, who would not meet my eyes, while Malia found a desk on the other side of the room near the front.

The bell rang and Mrs. Crandall and her evil assistant, Mrs. Young (who was, by my estimation, at least 150 years old), entered together.

"Quiet," Mrs. Crandall barked to the already silenced room. "There will be quiet in my classroom."

Mrs. Crandall took a long look around the room and stopped when her gaze found mine. "So you've returned to us, Miss Ashe. And just in time for a pop quiz. I do hope you did last night's reading."

"No, ma'am, I did not. I was a little bit preoccupied."

"Mm. So I've heard. I guess Mr. James's absence yesterday is excused after all."

The class gasped collectively, but not one person said a word.

"That's a terrible thing to say!" I started to stand, but I felt Ryan's hand on my shoulder.

I kept my bottom in my chair.

Mrs. Crandall quirked a bushy salt-and-pepper eyebrow as she watched our exchange. "Terrible? What is so terrible about the truth? I know you've had trouble with it from time to time, Miss Ashe, but I hardly think even you can say speaking the truth is a terrible thing."

She turned her attention away from me toward Malia. "Class, we have a new student. Malia Gervase. Oh yes, and one more thing. Before Mrs. Young passes out your pop quizzes, I must announce a seating change. Miss Ashe, please trade with Miss Gervase. Also, Mr. Charles left this for you." She handed me a sealed envelope. "Now, desks clear and pencils at the ready."

Chapter 11

That wasn't a pop quiz. That was a massacre. The only thing I answered correctly—the only question I answered period—was Name; and with Mrs. Crandall in charge of grading, I'd probably get points deducted for improper punctuation.

"Painful," Malia said as we left the classroom. "I bet she gets off on every wrong answer. Do you think maybe she and Mrs. Young grade the tests as foreplay?"

"Ugh. Thanks for the mental image. I can't believe she made you take the test."

"She told me I had plenty of time to do the reading so my absence was no excuse." Malia rolled her eyes. "Where are you headed now?"

"I have early lunch, then study hall."

"I'm exactly the opposite. I guess I'll see you for fourth-period trig."

"I'll be there," I said, pulling out Mr. Charles's note and an apple from my backpack. I was trying so hard to ignore the oppressive weight that was like liquid metal in my lungs. I felt Noah everywhere, and it was hard to breathe. Was he watching me, or was my guilt working overtime?

Students were filing into the cafeteria or outside to the courtyard with their lunches. I opened the envelope to find Mr. Charles's distinctive straight-lined handwriting. He never wrote in cursive.

AJ,
Come see me when you have some free time. I have something I want to discuss with you.
Mr. Charles

Perfect timing. I needed to do some research, anyway, and who better to help me than a teacher with an expertise in occult myth? If anyone could find information on the Serpentines, it was Mr. Charles. And while we were at it, maybe I could find out a little bit more about dichampyrs.

You know, just in case I was being stalked by one.

Mr. Charles's room was the farthest it could possibly be from the main building and still be considered on campus. I knocked and waited for his absentminded "Come in." As usual, he was hunkered over one of his giant tomes, studying each word as if God himself had written it.

"Mr. Charles?" I said when he didn't look up from the pages.

"Hmmm?"

"I got your note," I said. "So, here I am."

"Oh, yes, hey there, AJ. Come on in, have a seat."

He moved a stack of papers and books out of a chair next to his desk.

"What's up?" I asked.

"Well, I know you're doing all AP work this semester, and I was wondering if you had decided what you were going to do your thesis on."

Perfect. "Well, yes. Sorta. I was planning to research . . ." What? A family secret that is riddled in darkness and blood-sucking? No, that wouldn't work. "I was hoping to research a vampire myth."

"Excellent! You've always seemed interested in the occult part of my lessons, so I was hoping you would want to do something like that. Which is exactly why I wanted to see you. I love fate, don't you?" he said with a warm smile.

"I figure nobody else will do their paper on vampires, so maybe I'll stand out."

"Do you have something in mind, or would you like me to give you a topic? I have recently been studying some Celtic songs that I believe were once actually used as spells to cast away . . ."

"Have you ever heard of the Serpentines?"

He pulled off his reading glasses and raised his brows, eyes sparkling with curiosity. Nothing like a swim on a hot summer day, I thought as I nearly drowned in those deep green pools.

"AJ Ashe, where did you hear of the Serpentines?"

"It was a favorite scary story of my grandmother's," I lied. "She, um, loved to tell it on Halloween night to scare the bejeezus out of us before bed. Anyway, when I decided to write this paper, I did some preliminary research and found a little information. But I know there has to be more out there." Man, I tell one lie to a cop and, the next thing you know, I'm giving Pinocchio a run for his money. I wonder if that whole "lie bump" thing is true?

"As it happens, I do know a little about the Serpentines. Though I'm afraid probably not much more than what you've already discovered. Most of the Serpentine history was passed down orally, so I'm not sure that we'll find much in the way of written information," he said, watching me intently.

"Oh. Well, okay. I had to try. I'll probably see what I can dig up on my own. And if I can't find out anything else, maybe I'll switch my topic to those Celtic songs you were talking about."

"Switching topics might be easiest. But before you give up," he said, opening a desk drawer and riffling though it for a Post-it note and a pen, "call Jill Thompson. She has an antique bookstore over in Yellow Pine. If there's anything written down about the Serpentines, Jill's your gal. She has a thing for old vampire myths."

"Thanks, Mr. Charles." I folded the Post-it in half and slid it into my back pocket.

"You're welcome. Oh, and AJ? I'm glad you're running for president this year. Class officer always looks good on your college apps."

After school, I was forced to endure two hours of unending anguish that Coach called "soccer practice." Chinese water torture would've been more fun. We were out of shape and out of focus and, because of that, we did nothing but run. Like I hadn't done enough of that this morning.

But as much as it pained me, it did help me keep my mind off the feeling that Noah was watching me. My mind was really doing a number on me. Honestly, even if I had bitten Noah and turned him into a dichampyr, wouldn't I need to be there when he woke up? If I remembered the lore correctly, I would be his master. If he were left to fend for himself, he would be starving and wouldn't be able to control his need to feed. There would be a bloody trail of destruction following him until he was satisfied. He wouldn't be patiently watching me sleep, or jog, or have soccer practice.

Yeah, my guilt was definitely in overdrive.

Noah's family was so distraught over his missing body that they cancelled the memorial service. Not that I blamed them. Having your son's body misplaced must be pretty upsetting. So the school scheduled a service for Thursday this week in the auditorium. At least we'd get to say good-bye.

I pulled out my phone as I loaded my gear into the car. I had called Jill after speaking to Mr. Charles. She had agreed to stay open a little late for me tonight and said she might have exactly what I was looking for.

Now I just needed a partner in crime. I picked up the phone.

"*¡Hola!*" Bridget said when she answered. "*¿Cómo está usted?*"

"Guess you had Spanish today."

"*Sí.*"

"Well, how about you bring your brain back to English for a moment? That is, if you're in the mood for a road trip."

"Road trip? You bet. Where are we headed?"

"Just to Yellow Pine."

"That's not a road trip. That's a road stumble. What the hell is in Yellow Pine other than rednecks and fleas?"

"An antique book store. I am doing some fam—uh, some research for my AP thesis and the lady at the bookstore has something I need."

"AJ, as much fun as this trip sounds, I think I'm going to have to pass. I have a lightbulb I need to swallow tonight."

"You're not even gonna lie to me about needing to study?"

"Nah. Since when do I study?"

"Fine. I'll call Malia."

Malia was all about the road trip. Of course, she has always been a book lover like me, so this was really more up her alley, anyway. When we were younger, Malia and I would go to the library on purpose . . . you know, to get books to read. Bridget would tag along only because there might be a cute boy there. But I still wanted Bridget with me today. I'm sure if I had pushed it, she would've come, but probably it wouldn't have been worth the whining I would've had to listen to.

Yellow Pine is about thirty minutes from Valley Springs, and if Valley Springs is considered a small town, then Yellow Pine is positively microscopic in comparison. As the sign boasts, Population 84—not including the chickens. It has a Piggly Wiggly/Post Office. Next door is the Police Station/City Hall, and one block away is Jill's Antique Books and Tea Shoppe. You know it's a small town when the postmaster is also the butcher.

I parked in front of a pretty white Victorian house adorned with coral shutters and dragonfly wind chimes. The front porch creaked as we walked around to the bookstore entrance.

Jill opened the door before we rang the bell. She had short graying hair and a welcoming smile and wore her reading glasses on a beautiful multicolored beaded strand. She ushered us inside with a flurry.

"Hello, girls, welcome! Would you care for some tea?"

We both declined as she led us through a hallway cluttered with stacks of books piled to the ceiling. "Just ignore this mess. I've pulled the texts I think you're looking for."

Malia and I followed Jill past the entrance that led from the house to the store. We walked through the kitchen to a dark room in the back of the house. "This is where I keep my newly acquired stuff. It looks like a junk room, but I swear it's all organized chaos. I like to sort through everything here before I place it in the store. You can sit there." She pointed to a rickety card table. An old reading lamp cast a dim circle on the tabletop.

We took our seats as Jill reached behind a bookcase and flipped on an overhead light. Thank God. I was beginning to wonder if I needed to learn Braille.

"I got so excited after Morris—I'm sorry, Mr. Charles—called me."

"Morris?" Malia and I both started laughing. No wonder he kept his first name a secret.

"It's a very respectable name, so shush," Jill said with a slight smile as our giggles finally died down. "As I was saying, I got so excited because recently I bought an ancient chest that was rumored to have been carved for a vampire council." Her smile broadened. "I have a bit of an obsession with vampire mythology, so I collect—a lot," she said as an aside. "Anyway, in the chest I found a secret compartment. There was just one scroll hidden there, but I suspect there are more. When Mr. Charles mentioned the Serpentines, I just knew I could help. Take a look at this."

She gently lifted a yellowed parchment from a tube sitting on the floor next to the table. Its edges were no longer smooth and had darkened with age. The delicate paper made a sound like thick tissue as Jill rolled it flat onto the table.

The Serpentine S was imprinted in a dark red wax seal at the top. I knew the color had come from the blood of unwilling humans, and a chill washed over me. Malia touched the seal as if in awe.

"Wow," she whispered. "Touch it. It feels warm. Like it has its own energy."

"No way," I said. But when I looked down, my hand had acted alone, as if a magnet were pulling it. I started to fight the pull, then changed my mind and allowed my hand to touch the seal.

It is your destiny.

The voice in my head startled me—but not quite as much as the screaming did.

Their screams. Echoes of the victims who had been

sacrificed to create the mark. It was a blood seal imprinted with death and pain, and because of that, it was alive with the victims' energy.

And power.

I was equally repulsed and compelled. I tried to fight the impulse and pull my hand away, but instinct took over.

The force hummed through me, and as much as the sounds of death revolted me, the power tempted me. Called to me. All but invited me to be a part of it. Control it. Use it.

My gums tingled and I could feel my fangs as they began to descend. I closed my eyes to try to regain control, but instead, I seemed to fall into another world.

I was in a cold, damp cave, surrounded by fog. A hooded figure with piercing blue eyes stared at me. He smiled, but there was no warmth there. He held his hand out, and the screams seemed to fade into the background. There was chanting, but the language was foreign to my ears.

Focus on the white.

A new voice whispered.

Focus on the white.

I tried, but it was so hard. My fangs wouldn't ascend

and the world into which I had fallen wouldn't fade.

"Oh, look at that!" Jill said, removing my hand from the seal and breaking the trance I was under. My fangs shot back into my gums, and the hooded man with the blue eyes disappeared.

I couldn't really concentrate on what Jill was showing me because my head was still swimming a little. The humming faded, and all that was left was a breathless feeling, like I had been punched in the gut.

"That was weird," I muttered to no one.

Malia eyed me with a cocked brow. "You going all freakazoid on me?"

"No. I guess it's just my sinuses. You know, with all the dust in the air and everything." Okay, maybe not sinuses, but it was definitely a head trip.

I glanced at Jill, who was holding a magnifying glass over some text just below the seal.

"This is so strange," Jill said. "How did I miss this script? I'm usually more thorough than that."

"What does it say?" I asked.

"I'm not sure, it looks to be written in an ancient language. It's definitely rooted in Gaelic. I think I can decipher it—or at least come close." She placed the magnifying glass on the table. "I'll be in the back looking for the right text to help decipher the inscription. You girls can look as long as you like. Copy the text if you wish. Just don't take this with you. And be careful with it. This may be more valuable than I had originally thought."

"'The Lost has been found,'" I repeated to Malia as we drove into Valley Springs. "That was Jill's interpretation, right?"

"Yep. Pretty weird, huh?"

"Totally weird. I wish Bridget had been here with us. She would've loved that."

I pulled into Malia's driveway and parked. "What?" I asked when I saw the strained look on Malia's face.

"It's probably nothing. I'll see you tomorrow."

"No. It's not nothing. What are you keeping from me?"

Malia sighed. "It's just that Bridget has been acting way weird with me since I've been back. I'm sure it's that she's had you all to herself for so long and is readjusting to sharing."

"Ha-ha. Bridget is so not like that and you know it. I haven't noticed her acting any different."

"It could be me. Maybe *I* don't want to share *you*," she said, smiling. "I'm just so happy to be back. Thanks for calling me tonight."

Malia got out of the car and waved good-bye from the window in her living room. It *was* good to have her back. I picked up my cell and called Bridget.

"Hey, *chica*," she said, answering on the third ring.

"What took you so long to answer? You in bed already?"

"Not exactly. I was tucking Grady in for the night."

"You're such a slut! That's why you abandoned me tonight. You traded in your best friend for a booty call. I'm wounded."

Bridget laughed. "No booty call . . . yet. We were studying—for the most part."

"I thought you *never* studied," I reminded her with a snicker. "Whatever happened to friends first? Anyway, you missed a good time tonight. Malia went with me since you were too busy getting your 'study' on. We saw a pretty cool ancient document. And I swear some words just appeared on the scroll after we touched it."

She yawned. Loudly. "Sounds awesome. I bet that was so much more fun than sitting on Grady's lap with my tongue down his throat. How was Malia? She's been kinda weird since she's been back."

"Funny. She said the same thing about you. Are y'all

having trouble finding your friend groove?"

"I guess. Something doesn't feel right about her. It's like she's trying too hard to be *your* friend. Haven't you noticed?"

"She seems like the same old Malia to me, only taller and prettier," I said. "Hey, I'm home now, so I'll see you at school tomorrow."

"Later."

I clicked the phone off and stepped out of the car. My neck hairs stood to attention and goose bumps ran a race across my body as my gut clenched.

Someone was there.

I concentrated on my vision and scanned the surrounding area. It took a moment, but my very weak night vision finally kicked in. Why had I spent my entire life avoiding all things vampire?

I caught a flash of something over by the fence that separated the yard from the alley, but it moved too quickly. The wind picked up, carrying with it a whisper. Another voice. But this time, not in my head.

AJ.

My stomach lurched. I scanned along the fence until I saw another movement. A raccoon was perched on the railing, munching on a fresh piece of squash.

I guess I could hear animals talking to their food now. Boy, that's gonna be a useful ability.

"Aunt Doreen's gonna kick your ass if she catches you, Ricky Raccoon," I said with a laugh.

Obviously, I was paranoid. There was nothing out there. I had worked myself into a frenzy over the news that Noah's body was missing. Add that to a big dose of guilt, and you had me jumping to the biggest conclusion ever. What a moron.

But the goose bumps had not disappeared and my hairs were still standing on end. So I searched the woods once more just to put my unreasonable mind at ease.

A flash of color caught my eyes.

I glanced up to the large oak, sharpened my focus, and nearly threw up when I saw the face of Noah James staring back at me.

Chapter 12

It wasn't my guilt and I wasn't out of my mind.

Noah hissed, then lunged toward me from the tree. I stumbled backward, lost my footing, and fell on my butt in the driveway. He landed about ten feet from me.

I staggered to my feet and backed away, stunned and breathless. My body was shaking, like I had fallen through the ice on a frozen lake.

In a flash, Noah was behind me. He grabbed me by the arm but yelped and jumped back as if I had burned him.

I turned to face him.

"What do you want with me?" I asked, unable to

disguise the fear in my voice.

"Don't worry, AJ," he jeered. "*I'm* not going to hurt you . . . yet. But I'll be here. Watching. And even though I can't touch you, I *can* touch your family. So keep your trap shut or I'll feast on your sisters first and save your hot mom for dessert."

He paused and sneered. "I wonder if the twins taste alike."

And then he vanished into thin air. A yellow ribbon floated to the ground. I picked it up and panic seized my throat. It was a monogrammed hair band that belonged to Ana.

Well, the good news is, I wasn't schizoid. The bad news? My worst nightmare had come to life. Well, half-life.

I ran into the house, locking the door behind me in a panic. How would I keep Noah out of the house and away from my family? He wondered if the twins tasted the same? Ugh.

Panic flowed through me as I walked into the kitchen. Aunt Doreen was preparing a plate with a rare filet and a helping of mashed potatoes the size of my head.

"Perfect timing, dearie. I thought ye might be a bit famished."

"Wow. You're good," I said, hoping she was buying my "it's-all-cool" act. I sat my backpack down, glanced nervously out the kitchen window, and parked my butt at the island. "I can't believe I forgot to eat today." I *was* hungry despite the ball of nerves in my belly.

"It happens. Especially when ye've a lot on your mind."

"Mmmm. This is so awesome. Thanks." I had to force myself to stop obsessively glancing outside. I couldn't risk Aunt D noticing my jumpiness.

"I sprinkled a little sage and basil on your steak—to help you sleep a little better."

Okay, I either had Hefty bags under my eyes or Aunt Doreen dabbled in some form of medieval Scottish voodoo. How did she know I hadn't been sleeping?

The steak filled me up and cut any cravings I was having, but the mashed potatoes were like dessert. Why couldn't vampires just feed on loaded taters? Oh well, I always have been a dreamer.

I picked up my backpack and headed toward the stairs but stopped when I heard female giggling in the den. Then I heard Ryan's throaty laugh. My dinner suddenly felt like a boulder in my stomach.

I walked around the stairs and peered inside the room

to see Lindsey Rockport and Ryan huddled together on the floor.

Lindsey looked up with a slight smirk. "Hello, AJ. Would you like to join us? We're making my campaign posters."

Ryan flinched. "Hey," he said.

"You're running for president, too?" I asked before common sense could take over and stop me.

Lindsey's smile widened. It wasn't friendly. "Yes. I just assumed your brother told you." She placed her hand over his.

Gee, thanks, Lindsey. I'm pretty sure I would've gotten the hint without that little possessive move. My hackles went up immediately.

Ryan didn't move his hand. "I still plan to help with your posters, I promise."

"Aw, that's so sweet, Ryan. Too bad I hadn't planned to ask for your help. Y'all have fun." I turned and stalked up the stairs.

Then I slammed the door to my room, cranked up my Flyleaf CD, curled up next to Spike, and allowed myself a good cry.

Why couldn't I go back in time, erase the last four days, and start over? Things would be different. Ryan and

I would still be together. Noah would still be alive—and not in the undead way. And, most of all, I wouldn't know I was the descendant of some ancient evil clan of vampires.

It was bad enough knowing I was a regular vampire, thank-you-very-much.

Once my eyes finally stopped leaking, I pulled the shades on all my windows and noticed there were new window boxes full of ferns, basil, sage, and African violets. Clearly, Aunt D had been busy today. They were a nice touch and made the room feel homey. The fragrance calmed me a bit, taking my mind off the evil undead that loomed outside staring at me.

I slipped out of my clothes, placed my new necklace on the dresser, and ran a hot bath. Maybe I could soak my worries away. Not sure how I was gonna soak away my ancestry, or turn Noah James to dust with just a bath, but I was sure gonna try.

The steam from the water surrounded me like a fog, and the heat soothed me to the bone as my body seemed to melt into the water. I leaned back on my bath pillow and closed my eyes.

I missed Ryan. But, God, I was so angry with him. Not just over the Lindsey crap, which was enough of a reason, if you ask me, but over the Noah crap as well. He lied to me. And I lied *for* him.

They all lie, a voice whispered in my head.

Whatever. They don't all lie. I'm the one who lied to the cops, after all. Was that like perjury? No. I didn't swear an oath. I just lied to protect Ryan.

To protect yourself. Your history. Your destiny, the voice whispered again.

My destiny? What a joke. My destiny was supposed to be with Ryan. Or at least that's what I had thought. But no. My mother had to go and marry his father. I swear to God that life is just Fate's little chess game. She's a mean bitch, that Fate.

Destiny has two paths. Look to your past to find your future.

"AJ. AJ! Wake up," Mom said, shaking my shoulder. "How long have you been in here? You're freezing! Here." She handed me a towel. "Dry off and get dressed."

"What?" I asked, blindly obeying her. "What time is it?"

"Two A.M. Octavia called me a few minutes ago and told me I needed to check on you when I got home. She said she's still connected to you somehow. She said something about lots of guilt. Are you feeling guilty about something, honey?"

Shivering, I toweled off. "That's just freaky. I could've sworn I'd only been in the tub five minutes. But it must've been longer, since I was having some strange-ass dreams— with some weird voice. I guess Aunt Doreen's herbs did help me sleep."

"Are you okay?"

"Yeah. And I guess I'm feeling a little guilty about Noah. I can't help but wonder . . ." About why the undead Noah James was now stalking me? I shrugged into my pj's and jumped under my covers. I wanted to share my fears about Noah with Mom, but his threat hovered over me like a storm cloud. If I kept quiet, my family would remain safe. And even though I couldn't trust him, I also couldn't take that kind of risk. So I hedged.

"Plus I did some research today and I guess it kinda freaked me out a little."

"Honey, what happened to Noah was tragic, but it wasn't your fault. And I want you to be careful with your research, AJ. The Serpentines are not a clan we want to mess with."

"I'm only looking for information on the prophecy you were telling me about."

"Just tread lightly."

"Yes, ma'am. And thanks for not letting me drown,

Mom. I'm sorry about the fight we got into."

"Me too, honey. Me too." She leaned over and kissed my forehead. "Good night, my number one girl."

"Good night, Momma."

Chapter 13

The next morning was another day at Camp Chaos. The twins and Oz had commandeered another note—this one from a girl named Mary Beth.

Ana didn't get very far reading the note before Momma came in and stopped her. "We're not going to go through this every morning, do you understand me? If this happens one more time, it will mean no cheerleader tryouts for either one of you. Clear?"

They both hung their pretty blond heads in shame. "Yes, ma'am," they said in unison. But when Mom turned her back, they bared their fangs and silently hissed. Good thing Rayden was too busy putting together his backpack to notice.

"Do that again and see what happens," Momma said, not even looking up from the coffeepot.

She poured herself a cup of coffee, then made Rick a cup of tea—both to go. "I'm not on call tonight, so we're planning a family dinner. I want everyone here by seven. That's all of you, not just the girls."

Aunt Doreen bustled in from outside, carrying a basket full of vegetables. "I'm sorry, dearies, I lost track of time while working in the garden this mornin'. There's a loaf of fresh bread warmin' in the oven and a bowl of butter on the counter. Ye can take your breakfast with you to school."

"We have a garden?" Ana asked.

I opened the oven door. Steam hit me in the face, carrying with it the most awesome smell of fresh-baked bread. I pulled out the loaf and cut a large slice for myself.

"Aye, we have a garden. It's a bit past the giant tree in the back, on the other side of the picket fence."

"There was a raccoon out there having his way with a fresh squash last night," I told Aunt Doreen. "Hey, Rayden, are you riding with me today?"

"AJ, do you have a second?" Ryan asked as he walked into the kitchen.

"Nope. Don't you need to pick up your girlfriend this morning?"

I looked up to see Momma pretending to fuss with Rick's tea while she watched us out of the corner of her eye.

Ryan walked over to me and set his backpack onto the barstool. He laid his hand over mine, his eyes pleading. "Please? Can't we talk for just a second?" he asked, then silently mouthed, "Alone."

I buttered my bread and took a bite. "You get two minutes," I said with my mouth full. "Rayden, get in the car if you're coming with me."

Rayden grabbed his stuff and hustled out to the car. Ryan grabbed a napkin, tore off a piece of bread, and followed me to the driveway.

"Time's a-wastin'. What do you want?" I asked. I couldn't look at him. My heart ached every time I caught his gaze or smelled his scent. And no matter how pissed off I was at him, if he smiled at me, I'd be toast.

"I wanted you to know how sorry I am. Lindsey and I aren't *really* dating."

I laughed. "Who are you trying to convince? Me or yourself? If you're not dating, then what are you? Bene-friends?"

"It's not like that."

"It sure looked like that at the bonfire Saturday night. Of course, that was before you pummeled Noah and left him to die." Ugh. Why did I say that? "Shit, Ryan. I'm sorry. I didn't mean it."

"Yeah. You did. I had no idea that's what you thought of me."

"I said I was sorry. And I am." I reached for his hand, but he jerked it away. He may as well have slapped me.

"Listen, I just wanted to tell you that I did your campaign posters last night. I hope you like them." He stomped away.

God, I was a bitch.

I drove to school silently fuming. Rayden had the smarts to keep his mouth shut. Part of me wanted to carry through with this whole bitch thing and take my frustration out on him. But I managed to find some self-control.

I must be PMS'ing.

My almost legal parking spot was open, but I remembered Mrs. Blanchard's warning and decided to play nice. I didn't need any more drama in my life.

At least not today.

I parked off campus, and Rayden and I walked the two blocks to school. I took the time to quietly study Ryan's brother. He and Ryan were cut from the same cloth, as my Mema would say. Same color hair and eyes. Both with a dimple in their right cheek when they smiled.

Rayden was in that gawky stage where his arms and legs didn't quite fit his body. They'd both inherited their dad's height. Rayden was already taller than me, and Ryan was near six foot.

Funny. Ryan and I lived under the same roof, and I missed him more than if we lived oceans apart. I hated fighting with him and I hated not being with him.

I sighed.

"Hey, AJ," Rayden said as we entered the hallway of the English building. "You know, Ryan didn't hurt Noah."

"How do you know that?"

"I just do. And so do you. You're just mad at him right now. But you should cut him a break."

"Why should I do that, Ray? He's been an asshole."

Rayden stopped and looked at me. "Yeah, but this has been hard on him, too. Besides, would an asshole have spent all night doing this for you?"

"Doing wha—" I said before stopping dead in my tracks. "Whoa."

Whoa indeed.

The hallway was covered in posters. Fabulous,

elaborate, and beautifully done election posters.

All for me.

AJ for president. Vote for ~~Pedro~~ AJ. And my favorite: *AJ Ashe: Don't hate her because she's beautiful. Vote for her.*

Bridget ran up to me as I admired the hallway. "How the hell did you do this? How long have you been working on these posters? They're in every building!"

"Me? I didn't do this! Every building?"

"Yep. At least twenty in the science building. And I counted another fifteen in the corridor to the cafeteria. AJ, you had to have been here all night. How did you get into the school?"

"I didn't do this! Ryan told me he made me some posters last night . . ."

"No way he did these in one night. No friggin' way," Bridget sputtered.

And she was right. There was absolutely no way on earth that he could've done this in one night. They were so detailed. So perfect. And there were so many.

Even if he had made the posters last night, there was no way he could've hung them before school. He'd left just before I did this morning. There hadn't been enough time.

Bizarre.

Now I felt like a bigger bitch than ever. He'd worked his fingers off for me, and I had acted like an asshat.

The first bell rang and I started toward my locker to retrieve my books. Which is where Lindsey decided to corner me.

"You amaze me," she sneered from behind me.

I rolled my eyes and turned to face her. "Sometimes I even amaze myself."

"You're one of *those* girls, aren't you?"

"I'm sorry, Lindsey. I'm pretty smart, but I need you to be more specific here. If you mean I'm one of those girls with a vagina, then yes. I am." Sometimes I crack myself up.

"No. I mean if you can't have Ryan, you'll see to it that nobody else can," she said.

"It seemed to me that you had him just fine last night. And Saturday night. Is Lindsey afraid she might be second choice? Awww. Poor baby."

"You just couldn't get over the fact that he was helping me instead of you. Let him go already. Or do you wanna be known as the freak who's dating her brother?"

She had no idea what kind of freak I really was . . . and the tingling in my jaw was telling me to chill out quick or she was gonna learn real damn soon.

"First, Ryan isn't my *real* brother, he's my stepbrother. Second, Ryan and I aren't even together anymore. By all accounts, he's *your* bene-friend now. Enjoy him while you can, I've got to go." I slammed my locker shut, shouldered her out of my way, and headed to Advanced Anatomy. She had no idea who she was messing with.

Advanced Anatomy barely kept my attention this morning. Mrs. Simmons decided to do a recap of the cardio-vascular system, and today's topic was: blood. Well, if there's anything a vampire is familiar with, it's blood. So instead of actively listening, my thoughts alternated between apologizing to Ryan and getting rid of Noah.

I guess I zoned out in my quest for an appropriate apology, because the ringing bell surprised me. When I crammed my books into my backpack, a small bouquet of basil and sage tied together with a white ribbon fell out. Huh. Weird. I threw it back into my bag, zipped it up, and with a sense of dread weighing on my shoulders, headed for Mrs. Crandall's room.

Please, no more drama, I mentally chanted. *Please let there be a substitute*, I added.

Sigh. No luck.

Mrs. Crandall sat at her desk like she was the queen. Her prunelike face almost smiled when she saw me. No. It was too condescending to be a smile. It was a smug.

"Good morning, AJ," she said as I walked by her desk.

I stopped in my tracks.

"Good morning?" I asked.

I took my seat and waited for the bomb to drop. Nothing. I glanced around the room and saw Ryan's chair was empty. It wasn't like him to skip.

The whole class seemed to zone out during Mrs. Crandall's lecture. Not that she was ever really engaging, but today it seemed extra difficult to focus. I could feel myself nodding off, the lack of good rest finally taking its toll, when I heard that same sound from the other night.

Scritch, scritch, scritch.

My heart stopped and chills raced up my arms. I looked around to see if anyone else had heard it, but the rest of the class seemed near catatonic. I was the only person aware of any scratching.

Scritch, scritch, scritch.

I looked over at the window and froze.

Noah had left me a message.

I'm watching.

I could hardly breathe for the remainder of class. I spent the time wondering if I could get a restraining order against a dichampyr. I also kept waiting for Mrs. Crandall to call me out for being distracted, but she just kept on smiling, never saying a word. I couldn't believe I'd made it through a Crandall class without some sort of scarring. No bomb. No shrapnel. No phantom pains. Nothing.

I should be celebrating my victory, but for some reason, I was uneasy. Something just wasn't right.

Malia caught up to me, and we left class together.

"Is it me, or did she seem almost happy today?"

"Yeah. It creeped me out. Big-time."

"Oh my God! Me too! Maybe she and Mrs. Young got it on in the teachers' lounge before class. Maybe that was her 'afterglow' face."

"Ew!" I said, laughing. "I can't go there. You've got to stop giving me that mental picture. It makes me wanna poke out my mind's eye."

"Hey, where was Ryan today? I know he's here; I saw him this morning."

"I have no idea." I was still in shock and awe over the Dr. Jekyll side of Mrs. Crandall. Not to mention my little undead love note. I hadn't even begun to contemplate why Ryan had missed class.

Malia and I walked to my locker so I could exchange books for my third-period class. When we got there,

Bridget was waiting for us.

"I heard you and Lindsey got into it this morning," she said.

"Yeah. She came at me claws out. But I think I won the battle."

"Well, with these posters, it's likely you'll win the war, too. I haven't even seen one of hers yet."

"I know she has some," I said. "She and Ryan were working on them together last night."

"Ryan's been a busy boy, then," Malia added. "Sounds like he's trying to dip his wick into two vats of wax."

"I think this is really hard on Ryan," Bridget said. "And on AJ. I mean, one minute you're trying to get into each other's pants and the next you're supposed to be siblings. And AJ, you did tell him to move on. Is he still trying to get you to date him despite your parents' warning?"

"No. He seems to have his sights set solely on Lindsey now. Which is really for the best. How many people meet their soul mate in high school, anyway?" I said.

"You can do better than Ryan. He's a loser if he wants to date Lindsey," Malia said.

"He's not a loser," Bridget said.

"Gee, Bridget. I thought AJ was your friend," Malia said.

"All I'm saying is this situation isn't fair and he's doing the best he can. And you know AJ's my friend, Malia. That's not even funny."

"Okay, guys. Bridget is right. This situation is not fair. But Malia is right, too. If he wants to replace me with Lindsey, that's his problem. I was a total bitch to him this morning and I'm going to apologize for that, but he and I cannot be together." Even if one of his posters called me beautiful. I wonder if he used that same slogan for Lindsey.

"Um, AJ?" Bridget said, tapping me on the shoulder.

I turned to see Ryan coming down the hall with Mrs. Blanchard and Mr. Charles. Correction, he was being escorted down the hall.

His gaze caught mine, and he was silently pleading with me. Pleading for what? I guess I was about to find out.

"Ariel, we need to have a word with you," Mrs. Blanchard said.

"AJ, I'm so sorry." Ryan looked stricken. "I was just trying to help."

"Sorry for what?"

"Come along. You'll find out soon enough."

The crowded hallway parted like the Red Sea as I was escorted to an empty classroom.

"Have a seat."

Mrs. Blanchard was all business, which was pretty unusual. Not one smile or joke, which was not a good sign.

I looked over at Mr. Charles, but his face didn't give anything away.

"Before we begin, AJ, can you tell me if there is anything wrong with your school email account? Have you been having trouble?" Mrs. Blanchard asked.

"I dunno. I don't guess so. I haven't checked it yet. Why?"

"Do you remember the announcement that all school-related issues would be emailed to the students? We're cutting back on paper memorandums as much as possible, as part of the green initiative started by last year's student council."

"Oh, yeah. I totally think that rocks, too."

"Well then, why haven't you checked your email?"

"I guess with everything going on, I just forgot. Did I miss something?"

Mr. Charles sighed. "Betty, I really think we need to cut her a break. With Noah's death and everything."

My face warmed as it pinked. "Cut me a break for what? What's going on? I haven't done anything." Had I?

"Mr. Charles," Mrs. Blanchard chastised. "She's the only candidate who did not follow the rules. If we do as you suggest and 'cut her a break,' we are doing a disservice to those students who made sure they followed the rules to the letter."

"What rules? Would someone please tell me what I did wrong so I can fix it?" Dread fisted in my stomach again, but this time it was peppered with a whole bunch of panic. What could I have possibly missed?

"AJ, all the candidates for class officer were sent emails regarding the rules for this year's campaign. It seems that some of last year's posters got a little out of hand and the administration decided that all posters had to be pre-approved by the class sponsor before they were hung. And you did not get yours preapproved."

I breathed a sigh of relief. All this drama over campaign posters? Really? Posters I didn't even make. Or ask for? So I was gonna get my hand slapped for putting the posters up before I'd had them approved. I could live with that.

"I'm so sorry I didn't check my email. I had no idea and I promise to have any future posters approved before they're hung. Have you seen any with questionable content? I didn't make them, so I haven't even seen them all yet. I actually have no idea what they say." I laughed. It was a little forced, but I was trying to relax.

"We know Ryan made the posters and hung them for you this morning. He came to us when he found out we were going to ask you to take them all down."

"That's a little drastic, don't you think? I mean, I didn't even know he was gonna do the posters. And I hadn't read the email yet."

Mr. Charles sat down in the desk next to me. "AJ, we understand what happened. Ryan really went to bat for you. But the rules were established for a reason. And we can't bend on these. If we bend them for you, we have to bend them for everyone."

"Aren't they more like guidelines?" I asked hopefully.

"No, ma'am. They're chiseled in stone like the commandments."

"So I have to remove every one of the posters. There are, like, a hundred of them."

"According to Ryan, there are more like two hundred of them," Mr. Charles said.

Great. Could this day possibly get any worse?

Chapter 14

Of course it could get worse. Why hadn't I learned that by now?

The thought of removing all those posters was overwhelming to say the least. And even though I knew Ryan had the best intentions, part of me was a little pissed off at the fact that I had to clean up the mess.

Then my Catholic guilt punched me in the heart. Ryan had put up an astronomical number of posters for me because he cared. And if I were a betting girl, I would wager that he had barely even helped Lindsey.

Mrs. Blanchard handed me an excused tardy slip for my next class. I walked down the hall with every intention of removing the posters as I went when I realized they were already gone.

Huh.

Ryan must've told Malia and Bridget and they'd probably started removing the graffiti while I was in my "meeting." My friends are made of awesome.

I exited the English building and headed toward study hall with Coach Gerard. He is your typical grown-up jock and pretty cute, if you're into the bulk over brain kinda guy. He isn't stupid by any stretch of the imagination, but he also isn't the brightest bulb in the chandelier.

The door creaked when I opened it, and of course every head turned to look. I smiled and waved as I walked over to Coach G. and handed him my tardy slip.

"Mrs. Blanchard, huh? You get busted for illegally parking again, Ashe?" he asked with a laugh.

"Not this time."

"No, this time she broke a different rule," Lindsey said with a superior smile that made my eye twitch. "I think it's funny that she's running for class president when she can't even follow the election rules."

"Ouch. That hurt. I think I'm gonna cry. Can I borrow one of the tissues you stuff in your bra to blow my nose?"

The classroom filled with snickers and snorts as I took my seat. Thankfully, that shut Lindsey up. At least for a little bit.

Okay, I know I was being unfair to Lindsey. The situation we're in sucks, and frankly, I know I shouldn't be so mean to her. But every time she opens her mouth, I find myself projecting all my frustration and jealousy in her direction. I think if I could just "Hulk Smash" her one time, I'd be able to move on.

I couldn't sit still in class. Every few minutes I'd glance toward the windows to see if Noah had left me any more love notes. I tried to distract myself by reading, but the moment I'd start to relax, I would hear a low, gravelly laughter. It must've just been in my head, because nobody else seemed to notice.

Undead Noah was going to drive me out of my mind.

About ten minutes before the bell, the intercom buzzed with Mrs. Blanchard's voice. "Coach Gerard, will you please send AJ Ashe to my office?"

"Sure thing, Mrs. Blanchard. What'd you do now, Ashe?"

I slung my backpack over my shoulder and headed out the door. "I have no idea, but I'm sure I'll find out soon enough." I glanced over my shoulder to see Lindsey gloating.

I was really beginning to hate that bitch.

"Sit down, Ariel."

All business again. Not a good sign.

I sat down at the table in the corner of the office. "Is this about the posters again? They've already been taken down. . . ."

"No, ma'am. This is something entirely different and much more serious. We're waiting on a couple more people."

More serious? Oh, God. Was this about Noah? Had they discovered my secret? Would the world soon know that I was a descendant of an evil clan of vamps? Was there a vampire jail?

"Who are we waiting for?" I asked. But Mrs. Blanchard didn't have to say a word because my answer strode through the door carrying a file and wearing a sinister grin.

Mrs. Crandall.

I knew this morning's ray of sunshine act had meant something was up! Wonder what I did this time? Lord knows I couldn't be accused of cheating on yesterday's blood-forsaken pop quiz since the only question I'd answered was Name.

The old bat sat in the chair just to my left, and Mrs. Blanchard sat to her left, which placed her almost directly across the round table from me. And we waited a little longer.

Gee, nothing like sitting in a big vat of uncomfortable silence topped off with a thick dollop of tension.

Just when I started to open my mouth and ask one more time what the hell was up, the office door opened and in walked Ryan.

Hmmm. I thought this wasn't about the posters?

When Ryan saw me, it was apparent he was just as confused. He sat in the only empty chair and we both waited.

"We're very concerned about some possible impropriety involving you two," Mrs. Blanchard began.

Of course, when I heard "impropriety," my thoughts immediately went to making out with my stepbrother. And we totally hadn't done that since before the wedding.

Mrs. Crandall snorted. "That's one way to put it. Miss Ashe, do you care to tell me how it is that your test matched Mr. Fraser's test exactly?"

"Sure," I said. "Obviously the only question either of us knew the answer to was Name." I leaned over to Ryan.

"I guess you didn't study, either."

"No, I studied. I thought I did pretty well," he said, obviously still very confused.

"Well enough, I'd say," Mrs. Crandall responded, handing us our test papers.

What the—? I glanced at the paper, and sure enough, not only did our multiple-choice questions match, but the essay was almost word for word the same. And the handwriting was remarkably similar to mine.

"This isn't my test," I said, handing it back.

"It has your name on it and the essay is in your handwriting."

"It might appear that way, but that can't be my test. I didn't answer one question. Not. One."

"You're right. It seems you just helped yourself to Mr. Fraser's answers or he helped himself to yours."

"No. I'm telling you that I did not answer any questions at all. Not one multiple-choice question and certainly not the essay. I turned in a completely blank test," I said again, trying to disguise the panic that was creeping into my voice. "Besides, how would it have been possible for me to copy? You moved me across the room, remember?"

"That's a technicality. You seem to make a habit out of lying, Miss Ashe. And with your recent run-in with the law,

I have every right to wonder if you even know how to tell the truth at all." She turned her constipated face toward Ryan. "Mr. Fraser, were you aware that Miss Ashe was copying off of you? Did you assist her in any way?" she asked.

"No, but—"

"Did you copy off of her?"

"No! There's no way that we could have."

"I believe you. We received a tip that she might've used other means to cheat, but since your answers were so identical, we had to be sure. This is your one get out of jail free card, young man."

"But, Mrs. Crandall—" he protested.

"That is all," Mrs. Blanchard said, interrupting. "You can go back to class, Ryan. Thank you."

Okay, my cheeks were in flames. I'd bet my last breath that every drop of hemoglobin in my body was currently located in my face. I tried in vain to stop myself from speaking, but it was too late. I'm passionate like that, you know.

"My 'run-in with the law'? What is this? A John Wayne movie? There's a new sheriff in town, Miss Ashe. And Crabby Crandall thinks you're a liar," I mocked.

"Ariel Jane Ashe! Is that how I taught you to speak to your teachers?" my mother said as she walked through the door.

Oops. Somewhere along the way, I had become the Queen of Bad Timing. Any bargaining room I may have had was presently lying on the floor in a big pile of dust.

"Um, hi, Mom."

"Don't 'hi, Mom' me." She took the vacant seat and asked, "I assume I haven't been called away from the hospital for tea and cookies?"

"We've caught your daughter cheating again," Mrs. Crandall said.

"That's a lie! I wasn't cheating! Mom, I swear!"

Mom gave me that parental evil eye that always manages to shut the kid up no matter what.

"I'm assuming you have proof this time. Otherwise, I will be even more unhappy than I already am."

"Of course we do. We wouldn't have called you here otherwise," Mrs. Blanchard said.

"That didn't seem to stop you last year," Mom replied, and I started to relax. I shouldn't have been so worried. Mom was always in my corner. "Where is this proof?"

Mrs. Crandall smugged at me for the second time today and slid over the two test papers. I was getting really sick of seeing that condescending look of hers. "One of two things happened. She either copied off of your stepson, or she used a cheat sheet of some kind."

"You saw it happen?"

"Well, no. But the answers are identical."

"Mom, I—"

She shot me another look and then glanced over the tests.

"And naturally you think they cheated. Why isn't Ryan being called to the carpet? Or have you notified his father?" she asked.

"Well, we've determined that Ryan was unaware of your daughter's cheating. We have given him a pass, much like we gave Miss Ashe a pass last year."

I cringed. It didn't matter if I had cheated. Mrs. Crandall was still holding a grudge from last year. I was burnt toast.

"What's the next step? I'm assuming you called me here because there will be disciplinary action?"

Et tu, Mother? "Mom!" I yelled. "You know I didn't cheat!" How could she do this to me?

"I'm afraid so, Mrs. Fraser. We have a zero tolerance rule when it comes to cheating. There's too much evidence here to ignore. AJ admitted she didn't study for the quiz—"

"No. I admitted that I only wrote my name on the paper before I turned it in," I retorted. Tears were stinging my eyes, but I refused to let them fall. I faced Mom. "I didn't answer one question. I swear it."

A light knock on the door interrupted my crucifixion. Miss Mandy entered holding a lock and another piece of paper. She handed both to Mrs. Blanchard and sent me an apologetic glance.

"Do you recognize this lock, Ariel?" Mrs. Blanchard asked.

"Um, it looks like the one from my locker. Why?"

"It *is* the one from your locker. And do you want to tell me what we found in there today?"

"Let's see. I'm sure you found all my posters of Shia LaBouef, the 'Hi, I'm a Mac' dude, and David Beckham. Why did you go through my locker? I'm confused."

Confused didn't even begin to cover it. If I took a minute to really think about it, I'd be pissed.

"We received an anonymous tip that you might be in possession of the test key. We searched your locker and guess what?" Mrs. Blanchard waved the test key in the air like a flag.

"It's a lie! Mom, I swear I've been set up! I never saw the test key. I didn't even know there was one! You have to believe me!" I was begging, and it wasn't pretty.

"Well, Miss Ashe," Mrs. Crandall interrupted. "It'd be easier to believe if you didn't have a history of lying. We have last year's incident, and more recently, the rumors around school are that you lied to the police about Noah James. How do you expect us to believe you now? Especially with such strong evidence against you."

My eyes popped open in wide surprise. Why did she think I had lied to Officer Littleton? I mean, I had, but that wasn't the point. The point was, how did Crabby Crandall know?

"Well, I guess I know why you were feeling guilty yesterday. I'm sorry, AJ. This is the bed you made, now you have to lie in it," Mom said.

My heart sank when Mrs. Blanchard uttered the words "three-day suspension." How was that going to look on my college transcript?

As we were leaving, Mrs. Blanchard added, "And AJ, because of your suspension, you can no longer run for president. I'm sorry, but class leaders have to be positive role models."

The idea that Little Miss Unshine could be a more positive role model than me was ludicrous.

Mom and I left the office in silence. I had never been so disgusted in my life. I had totally been set up and nobody believed me. I wasn't a liar. Okay, so I *had* lied to protect Ryan, but that was it. And how had that gotten around the rumor mill so fast, anyway?

Then I remembered. Cody Littleton was Crabby Crandall's nephew. Hello, AJ. How about a big bite of "duh cake."

"AJ, you get your car and take your ass home. No. Wait. Before you go home, I want you to go to Pot and Kettle and tell Rick what happened. I have to get back to a patient or I would do it myself. And then we'll discuss this tonight. As a family. Be there for dinner."

"Tell Rick? Are you kidding me? Why?"

"Because he's your father now."

It had always been just Mom and me. In truth, we had been more like sisters than mother-daughter. Now she wants to go all parental on me?

"No, Mom. He's the guy you married. I like Rick, I do. But I am not going to his company and tell him anything."

"You will. This is how families work. Now go. And AJ, once you get home, you stay there. Do you understand me?"

"Fine," I snapped. "Mom? You do believe me, don't you?"

She looked at me with soft blue eyes full of disappointment. "Honey, I don't know what to believe anymore."

Chapter 15

I sat in the parking lot of Pot and Kettle for at least ten minutes before I went inside. I didn't want to go into Rick's office and tell him that I had just been suspended from school on the suspicion that I had cheated on my test with his son.

"It's now or never," I muttered.

Pot and Kettle was a cookware manufacturing company specializing in, you guessed it, pots and pans. I had been inside the headquarters a few times before. Since it was the Fraser family business, Ryan worked there in the summer, so I kinda knew my way around.

The offices were in an old stone house that looked like it had been around since medieval times. It wasn't a castle, but it definitely would've been considered a "manor."

The large plank wood and wrought-iron door creaked when I opened it. Rick's secretary, a pretty woman named Heather, smiled when I entered. She reminded me of one of those calendar pinup girls from the 1950s.

"Hello, AJ. We've been expecting you," she said.

"Hi. I guess my mom called?" I asked.

Heather just smiled and picked up the phone. "Rick, your daughter is here."

His daughter. Well, I guess that was better than being called his stepdaughter. Still, he hadn't even been married to my mom a week. I wasn't really ready to be called his daughter yet.

"He'll be here in just a second," Heather said. "Can I bring you a soda or something while you wait?"

"No, thanks," I said just as Rick walked into the room.

His smile was warm. "Come on back, AJ," he said, his faint Scottish burr tickling my ears.

Rick draped his arm across my shoulders and led me down the hallway and up a spiral staircase to a large room that would've been the master bedchamber had this actually been a medieval home.

The walls were rock and the floors were wood plank.

There was a giant stone fireplace to the right, with a large cast-iron pot suspended in the center. Huge windows with heavy plaid draperies tied back with rope lined every wall.

Rick sat at his oak desk in the middle of the room. "You have something you want to talk about?" Rick asked.

"Um, yeah. That pot looks like a witch's cauldron," I said, pointing to the fireplace.

Rick smiled. "It's a great conversation piece, don't you think? But I don't think that's what we really need to discuss right now, is it?"

I sighed. Obviously I wasn't going anywhere anytime soon if I didn't start talking.

"I was suspended from school today," I blurted.

"I see."

"And it was totally bogus. They said I cheated off of Ryan, but I didn't—we don't even sit near each other. Then they found the test key in my locker, but I didn't put it there! I mean, what kind of idiot would keep the evidence on school property?" I was talking so fast, everything I said came out in one breathless sentence.

"That does seem rather careless," Rick said.

"I know, right? And I'm not that stupid. I didn't even study for the test because of all the stuff with Noah. I was tired and cranky and I just wrote my name on the paper and turned it in. I don't know how or by whom my test was altered, but I know Crandall saw that it was blank when I turned it in. I was totally set up and nobody believes me. You believe me, right? Will you help me with Mom?"

"Whoa. Hold on for a second. That puts me in a bit of a tough spot, don't you think?"

My lungs deflated a little. "I guess. But if you're not gonna help me—"

"I didn't say that. We'll get this sorted out, I promise. But I do need to talk to Ryan and to your mom before I figure out what to do."

So much for having Rick in my corner. He walked me out to my car, and waiting in the parking lot was Sheriff Al Christopher.

I saw him immediately but pretended I hadn't noticed him. I opened my car door and started to get in, but the good sheriff was right there to stop me.

Sheriff Christopher was a big guy with graying coal black hair and apple pie cheeks. When he smiled, he seemed like the greatest guy in the world. But today, there were no smiles—in fact, he looked pretty grim.

"Hello, Sheriff, how can I help you today?" Rick asked.

"I'm here to speak to AJ. You're welcome to stay around if you'd like, Mr. Fraser, but you're not required to," the sheriff said.

"I think it would be best if she had a parent present, thank you."

"AJ," Sheriff Christopher said. "I've got a few more questions for you about Noah."

"Okay. Maybe come by tonight when my mom is around? I don't feel comfortable answering questions without her."

"Well, we can do that, I suppose. But since your stepfather has offered to be here, it makes me wonder if you're not putting me off because you're guilty of something. But you go ahead and call her if you'd like."

I sighed—heavily. Then I looked at my watch. "No. She's with a patient right now. And I have nothing to feel guilty about."

"If you're lying to protect Ryan, you do," the sheriff said.

"Wait a minute, what are you saying, Sheriff?" Rick asked.

"I'm just asking questions, Mr. Fraser. Now AJ, are you lying to protect your boyfriend?"

"He's my brother," I said, sliding a glance to Rick.

"And I'm not a liar, Sheriff."

"Darlin', you and I both know that's not true."

I swallowed as he stared at me with those all-knowing, almost silver eyes. Seriously, was I wearing a scarlet L?

"I don't know what you're talkin' about." I broke away from his gaze and got into my car.

"Really?" he asked, stopping me from shutting the car door in his face. "Because I just left your school and they told me you'd been suspended for cheating. Isn't cheating a form of lying?"

"I didn't cheat! I was set up."

"You and every other asshole in prison."

"Excuse me?"

"Now Sheriff, that was unnecessary," Rick said.

"My apologies. I'm just saying, darlin', the 'I was framed' defense is a little overused."

"Whatever. Just tell me what you want so I can go home and pout alone."

He chuckled at that, and his apple pie cheeks reddened a little more. I relaxed a bit. At least when he smiled, I didn't feel like he was about to arrest me.

"When Officer Littleton questioned you, you told him that Noah got rough with you. Is that correct?"

My face turned hot in an instant. Why did I have to

re-answer these questions? It was bad enough I had to tell the story in front of Mom, but now I had to talk about my almost sex life in front of my stepfather? Just. Shoot. Me. Now.

"Would you like me to leave?" Rick asked. "I don't want to make this any more difficult than it already is for you."

I nodded sheepishly.

"Sheriff, don't bully her. She's had a rough day." Rick squeezed my arm and hesitated, like he didn't want to leave. He gave me a forced smile, attempting to reassure me, then left me alone with the hungry wolf.

"Don't worry, AJ. I've heard everything in this business. Now just tell me, as best you can, what happened."

I relayed the sordid details, all the way down to Noah forcing me to grab his crotch.

"And you reported that you bit his tongue when he forced himself on you. Correct?"

"Yes. Couldn't you have just confirmed this with a text message or an email? My story isn't gonna change no matter who asks me."

"Your friends came along right after you bit Noah. Then you and the girls left together, right?"

"Right."

"Okay, so Ryan stayed back with Noah. What happened next?"

"Wait. No. Ryan left with us, too."

Sheriff Christopher raised his eyebrows and stared at me.

"What?" I asked.

"Sounds like your story's changing, darlin'."

"No. It sounds like you're trying to trick me. We all left together. Just like I told Cody." Was it too late to get Rick to come back? Suddenly I felt like I needed a dad, any dad.

As he was making another notation in his lie detector book, my phone rang. It was Mom.

"I just called the house and Aunt Doreen said she hasn't seen you yet," Mom said before I could even say hello.

"That's because I'm still at Pot and Kettle getting the third degree from the sheriff."

"Put him on the phone."

I held the phone out to Sheriff Christopher and said, "Um, Mom wants to talk to you."

He took my pink RAZR. "Hello?"

Silence.

"Yes, ma'am."

"Yes, ma'am."

"Yes, ma'am. I understand. You have a good day, Dr. Fraser."

He handed me the phone, closed his notebook, and said, "Thanks, AJ. We'll talk again soon."

I put the phone back to my ear. "Mom, whatever you said to him to make him go away, I totally love you for it."

"Don't thank me just yet, Ariel Jane. Now, get home and don't move until I get there. And trust me, you don't want to test me on this. Are we clear?"

Clear as fucking glass.

My phone started ringing the moment school was out. Word of my suspension traveled fast, it seems. I was none too happy to hear from my soccer coach that I was suspended from practice and the first game of the season. If you asked me, I was being punished twice for the same crime.

A crime I didn't commit, thank-you-very-much.

When Bridget and Malia called, I told them to get their butts to my house ASAP so we could work out some sort of plan.

What we were planning exactly was still a mystery.

But we were gonna plan something, come hell or high water.

I went downstairs to gather sustenance from the kitchen and ran smack into Ryan.

"AJ, I'm so sorry."

"Whatever."

"Seriously. I tried to go talk to Mrs. Blanchard this afternoon, but she wouldn't let me. I know you didn't cheat."

"I'm learning the truth doesn't really matter anymore. Thanks for trying, though. And even though it sucks that I can't run for office, thanks for the posters. They were awesome. I'm sorry I couldn't help take them down."

Ryan shrugged out of his backpack, then walked over to me and wrapped me up in a hug. I melted into him. The tears I'd been fighting all day finally broke free, streaming down my cheeks. "They're all down now, don't worry."

He pushed my hair out of my face and kissed my cheek. My heart stopped for a second and time crackled to a halt as we stared at each other. The air was so thick, it was almost tangible as he leaned in and touched his lips to mine, never breaking our stare. I realized I didn't want to stop him, even though I knew the repercussions would be messy. I was just so tired of pretending.

Pretending I didn't still care for Ryan.

Pretending that my family wasn't being threatened by a dichampyr.

Pretending I was strong enough to handle everything all by myself.

And, most of all, pretending I wasn't scared to death of all of the above.

Nothing mattered at that moment but Ryan's mouth on mine. I pushed away my doubts about his involvement with Noah and my need to protect him no matter the cost. I ignored the finger of fear that touched my spine, warning me that Noah was out there watching. I disregarded the bells in the back of my head that screamed this was a bad idea, and I tried to forget the burning birthmark on my neck and just let it happen. I opened my mouth and Ryan deepened the kiss. My heart hitched to speed-racing, and chills washed over me as I lost myself to him completely.

"Kinky," Rayden said, slamming the kitchen door behind him. "Pa! Ryan's kissin' his sister again!" he yelled, turning on a thick country accent that was more exaggerated than Jessica Simpson's version of Daisy Duke.

"Very funny, dickweed," Ryan retorted, but I saw him

look over Rayden's shoulder to make sure his dad wasn't around.

Thankfully, Rick wasn't there.

Unfortunately, Lindsey was.

That girl was beginning to piss me off.

She stood there, with her eyes large and appropriately shocked and her mouth hanging open like a wide mouth bass.

"Seriously, Ryan?" she asked before she turned and stormed off.

"I'm sorry," he said to me as he went after her.

I grabbed him by the arm. "You're really gonna go after her? After that kiss?"

"AJ, I'm *so* sorry. I have to."

"You're sorry. On that point, we both agree."

Thank God Malia and Bridget walked through the door, otherwise I would've slapped the skin off Ryan's face.

"Uh-oh. Looks like we just missed the fireworks. I didn't know it was the Fourth of July, did you, Malia?" Bridget said, trying, and failing, to lighten my mood.

Malia just shot Bridge a look and ran over to my side. "Ignore the court jester, honey. What's wrong?"

"Nothing. I just need to get out of here," I said.

"Do you think that's such a good idea? Didn't you tell me when I called that your mom threatened dismemberment if you left the house?" Bridget asked.

"Pretty much," I said, trying to laugh. "But I don't care. I can't be here right now."

"Let's go, then," Malia said, pushing me out the door.

As we were piling into Malia's black SUV, Ana, Ainsley, and Oz were dropped off by this week's carpool mom.

"Is it true?" the twins asked in unison. "Did you really cheat and get suspended?"

Oz didn't say anything. He just stared at Malia.

When she glared back at him and said, "Boo!" he ran off.

"I didn't cheat, but I did get suspended. Listen, Mom told me not to leave, but I have to get outta here. Do me a favor and cover for me? Please? When Mom comes looking for me, pretend I'm in bed asleep? Can y'all do that?"

They both ran over and hugged me big. "Sure," they said.

"Oh, and one more thing. When Ryan gets back, be sure that my stereo is blasting with something angsty. And if it slams his current choice of a girlfriend, you'll get bonus points."

They both giggled and wandered into the house singing, "Don't ya wish your girlfriend was hot like me; Don't ya wish your girlfriend was a freak like me; Don't ya?"

Freak. That was the truth of it all right there. Lindsey was a lot of things, but there was no way in hell she was a freak like me.

Chapter 16

"Where to?" Malia asked as she spit gravel with the tires and pulled out of my driveway.

"I haven't thought that far ahead. Anywhere is better than here," I said, glancing out the window. He was there. I couldn't see him, but he was there.

"AJ, I think this is a bad idea. I don't mean to be a prude here, but your mom is gonna be pissed off and you'll be screwed," Bridget said.

She was right, but honestly, I didn't care. "I know, Bridge. Hopefully, the twins will be able to cover for me and if Momma finds out, well, I'll just deal with it when it happens. Does anyone have any aspirin? My birthmark hurts so much right now, it feels like it's growing."

Malia looked at me a little funny and handed me her purse. "Help yourself."

We drove through town for about an hour, stopping at the local Sonic rip-off for chili-cheese dogs and vanilla malts.

"Hey, I just realized the time," Bridget said. "I've got to get to Grady's house. We're studying tonight."

"You seem to 'study' a lot these days." I laughed.

"Ha-ha. I'll have you know we really do study. It's just, sometimes I'm sitting on his lap at the same time."

I shot her a look.

"*Fully clothed*. We haven't gone there yet. And I don't plan to for a while. I really like him," she said with a goofy little smile. "Malia, can you take me back to school so I can pick up my car?"

Malia's phone rang, so she just nodded as she answered the call. "Hello?"

We could hear someone talking frantically on the other end, but we couldn't make out the conversation.

"That's so cool! We'll be right there!"

She closed her phone and started the car. "AJ, that was Mr. Charles! He said he tried to call you but he just got your voice mail. The bookstore lady found two more scrolls and he thinks he's discovered something in them."

"Awesome. Where is he?" I asked, digging my phone out of my purse. "Hm. He must've dialed the wrong number. I don't have any missed calls. How did he get your number?"

She looked at me. "He's the class sponsor. Why wouldn't he have my number? Anyway, he's at school. So we'll take Bridget to her car so she can have her face time with Grady and I'll go with you to Mr. Charles's room."

Bridget's face took on a severe expression. "AJ, I know I sound like a broken record here, but—" she managed to say before Malia interrupted her.

"But arc you sure this is a good idea? Wah, wah, wah! When did you become such a damn goody-goody?" she askcd.

"I'm not a goody-goody. But she's suspended! If she gets caught on campus for any reason, her suspension could be doubled, or worse, she could be expelled! That's a bigger freakin' deal than just not listening to her mom, Malia. Jesus. When did you become such a bitch?"

"Okay, you two. That's enough. Bridget, I'll be with Mr. Charles, who I'm sure will come to my defense if I need him to. Besides, this is for my thesis, so it's important. And hell, I'm already in this much trouble, what's a little more? Now, do you wanna come with us? I'd really like you to be there."

I did want her there. This was important to me, and even though I couldn't tell her why it was so important, I needed my best friend with me.

Bridget sighed. "I want to, I really do. But we have a quiz tomorrow, and I know you think we're not studying, but we are. Mom has already told me I don't get to go to Spain with the Spanish Club if I don't make straight A's. So I have to study. Will you fill me in tomorrow? Every detail?"

Disappointment sizzled in my belly. "Of course."

She leaned over the backseat and hugged me, then whispered in my ear, "Be careful. I really think this is a bad idea."

I nodded and squeezed her neck once more.

"Who put a bug in her butt?" Malia asked as she drove around to the far end of campus.

"She's just worried because I haven't been myself this week," I replied. Have I ever really been myself?

"No shit. It's kinda hard to be yourself when you're being questioned for murder."

"Stop being so dramatic. I'm not a suspect. They just *suspect* I'm covering for Ryan. Which I totally am, even though I don't know why. He might be an asshole, but there is no way he hurt Noah like that."

"Are you one hundred percent sure about that?" she asked, parking her car right next to Mr. Charles's.

Despite the fact that he had motive, had the time, and had bruised and bloodied knuckles, I *was* surprisingly sure he had not hurt Noah. "One thousand percent sure."

It was strange, this lack of doubt. I couldn't explain it other than to say that I knew he was innocent like I know I'm a vampire. It's just inside me. And I had to fight for him, even if Ryan couldn't fight for me.

Mr. Charles met us at the door wearing a big dimpled smile. I don't know how he hadn't managed to find himself a wife. He must be high maintenance or gay.

No way was he gay. No way.

"Hey, ladies. C'mon in."

The heavy door slammed shut behind us, chasing the echoes of our footsteps with its hollow clang.

We walked past Mr. Charles's classroom, into a lounge area. "The lighting is better in here," he said.

"So Jill found some additional scrolls?" I asked.

"Yes. She called me last night saying she'd found another secret compartment in the chest and two more scrolls. It's all very exciting, isn't it?" Mr. Charles said.

The three scrolls were spread out across one long table. Malia and I sat down and Mr. Charles pulled out a laser pointer. "Okay, Malia reported that the writing beneath the seal seemed to just appear when you guys touched it. Does it look the same now?" he asked.

"Yeah. It looks like it did after we touched it," I answered. "Jill said it roughly translated to 'the lost has been found.'"

"Yes. That's pretty much what it says. And y'all didn't touch the other scrolls?" he asked.

"No. We didn't even know there were other scrolls. Besides, I was kinda freaked out, so even if there had been others, I wouldn't have touched them."

Malia shot Mr. Charles a look and nodded. "It was weird. AJ seemed to zombie-out on me."

"You had a physical reaction to it?"

"I guess I did. It just seemed to hum when I touched it. I know that sounds weird and I know you probably don't believe me, but that's what it felt like."

"But I do believe you, AJ. I've come across similar phenomena in my research. If there's one thing my studies of the occult have taught me, it's to never underestimate the power of magic. The modern world has lost its connection to old-world magic. But you can't lose touch with genetics. AJ, didn't you say that your grandmother used to tell you stories about the Serpentines? Is that why you're so interested in vampires?"

"Um, yeah," I said, twisting my hair around my finger. That had totally been a lie. But I suppose if I had known my dad's mom, she probably would've told me stories about my evil ancestors.

He smiled and, I swear to God, I saw his eyes twinkle. "I want to do a little experiment. Do you trust me?"

Right now, Mr. Charles was about the only person I could trust. Mrs. Blanchard had gone to the dark side with Crabby Crandall. Ryan was off chasing Lindsey's skirt. Bridget was choosing Grady over me. The cops were hot on my trail, and even my mom didn't believe a word I uttered. "I guess I do."

"Okay, I want you to touch the seal of the second scroll."

"I dunno, Mr. Charles. I'm telling you, it was really freaky. I don't wanna feel that again."

"I know it must've been scary. But I'm here and I won't let anything bad happen to you."

"You should've gone into sales," I said. I smiled, but a current of nerves seized my lungs, making it hard to breathe.

Malia's phone rang. "It's my grandmother," she said, looking at the caller ID. "I'll be back in just a second."

Mr. Charles wrapped a strong arm around my shoulders. "Do you want to wait for her?"

I sighed. "No. Let's just do this while I have my nerve up. I'll give her the play-by-play when she gets back."

Mr. Charles led me closer to the second scroll and stood with me as I looked over the parchment. The air around me tingled with electricity, kind of like it did when I was with Ryan. My birthmark didn't burn this time, though it did ache with an intensity that made my knees buckle. Mr. Charles steadied me, and I tried to pull away as the magnetic force of the scroll began to tug me forward.

"Don't be frightened," he whispered.

I wasn't frightened. A sense of calm washed over me like a warm bath. I closed my eyes and held my hand to the seal. Shocking heat seared my skin, and though I sensed the burn, it didn't hurt at all.

And this time the voices spoke to me.

This is the call to power. Let us bring you to life.

The fire cooled beneath my hand, but did not burn out.

Feel the darkness; feed in light; with your blood, reclaim the rite.

The chant purred through me and I gave myself to it. I fell into the other world again, and this time I was in a room full of jewels. I was sitting on a throne; people were bowing before me. There was a man, a beautiful man, with eyes like sapphires and a smile so perfect, he didn't seem real. But he was real, and he sat on a throne next to me. We were holding hands, and he was smiling. When I looked into his eyes, I knew he was promising me the world.

The desire for power I had felt in the bookstore barreled to life inside me again. My body pulsed with yearning. Deep inside, I felt a part of me tug away from what was offered. There was something in me, frail and quiet, but firm in its belief that what I saw, what I felt, was evil, but it was so weak, it didn't stand a chance to win.

Just when I had decided the picture before me was real, a stinging slice to my palm jolted me away from fantasy land and back to my reality.

"Jesus!" I screamed. "What the hell was that?" I said before I remembered I was standing with a teacher and probably, no matter how cool that teacher was, I should watch my mouth around him.

"It's okay, AJ," Mr. Charles said, wrapping my now bloody hand in a paper towel. His face was pale and his hands were shaking. His words were laced with nervous excitement. "I had to force your hand off the seal. It . . . it was like it wouldn't let go of you. I finally wrenched it away, unfortunately, at the cost of some of your skin. I'm sorry. I obviously let it go on longer than I should have."

Still a little dazed, I looked at the blood soaking through the paper towel. It was almost like I had just run five miles on empty. I was light-headed, my legs were wobbly, and I saw stars when I closed my eyes.

Mr. Charles supported me, and I leaned in to him to steady my footing. When I opened my eyes, I noticed there were drops of blood on the document. "Oh no! Jill is gonna kill me! I can't believe I bled all over an ancient scroll."

"I'll handle Jill. She'll be fine with it. Oh my God, AJ. Look!" He pointed at the droplets of blood and we watched as more writing appeared.

"It's like it feeds on your blood," Mr. Charles said.

"Can you decipher that?" I asked.

"This is amazing! Truly fascinating!" He ran out of the room and I followed him. In his classroom, he marched over to his junked-up desk and began to shuffle through the papers and books. He opened drawers, moved the chair out of the way, and searched beneath the desk. "I was just using it. Where has it gone? Think, Charles, think. Where were you last?" Mr. Charles stood there among the wreckage tapping his chin and talking to himself like a cartoon professor.

"That's right!" he muttered after a few seconds. He took off back to the room we had just come from. "In all my excitement, I forgot that I had prepared for this possibility by bringing the text into the room with me. I would lose my head if it weren't attached."

He picked up the old book and flipped through the pages. He had already bookmarked some of the pages in advance with Post-it notes. After skimming several premarked pages, he finally seemed to find what he was looking for.

His brow furrowed as he glanced from scroll to book, trying to translate the ancient script.

"This is very perplexing," he said.

"What is?" Malia asked, finally returning from her phone call. "Did I miss anything?"

"The translation reads: 'One has been found. There is another.'"

"What does that mean?" I asked.

"I have no idea." Mr. Charles peered at me. "AJ, is it possible that you're somehow a descendant of the

Serpentines? With your grandmother telling the story, it stands to reason—"

"Me? A descendant of an evil clan of vampires?" My heart jumped into overdrive. I trusted Mr. Charles, except . . . even I wasn't that stupid. And I certainly couldn't let him guess. Dammit! Why did I make my interest in the Serpentines family based?

"Mr. Charles, I know you're really into occult myth and all, but seriously, vampires aren't real. I think you've been walking that line between fantasy and reality a little too long."

"My dear, every myth has a foundation in truth." His smile was warm and friendly. "I know it's a scary thought, but think about your family history. It would be an amazing discovery, don't you think?"

"If I had a vampire in my family? No. That would *so* not be cool. Besides, it's not possible. I thought vampires couldn't see themselves in mirrors or burn in daylight. Wouldn't I know if I had been bitten?"

There you go, AJ. Play it off.

"There's more to vampires than what you hear from tall tales. Vampires can be born. They aren't just bitten and turned. And they've evolved way beyond the mirror and daylight thing. In order to survive, they've had to adapt. That's why stories about them keep changing."

"You believe in vampires?" And, more to the point, how the hell does he know all that? Was Mr. Charles a vampire? No. There was no way.

"I believe in a great number of things, AJ. Now, tell me about your family history."

I squeezed my injured hand shut and took a deep breath. "Mr. Charles, I lied. It wasn't my grandmother who told me that story. I've never even met my grandmother. I actually picked up the story from a conversation I overheard at Starbucks when I was in Memphis. I thought it would sound more authentic if I said it came from my family."

Wow. Lying seemed to be the only thing I could do right these days.

"Why didn't you tell Mr. Charles the truth?" Malia asked as she drove me home.

"I did."

"AJ, there is no way you heard that story at Starbucks. C'mon. You can tell me."

Actually, I couldn't. I couldn't tell anyone. Mom had always warned us about confiding in people about "our truth." I didn't want to take the chance that I would lose the only people I really could trust right now.

"It's true. I overheard it the day before school started, when Mom and I went shopping. I thought the story was cool and I decided I would research the Serpentines for my thesis. I figured if I couldn't find anything on them, no harm."

"And then you hit the mother lode with Mr. Charles?" she asked.

"Yeah. I knew if anyone could help me, he could. I swear he knows everything about the occult."

"Maybe there's a reason he believes in vampires," Malia offered.

I let that thought ricochet through my mind as Malia pulled into the alley behind my house. My mom's car wasn't in the driveway, which actually surprised me. But I couldn't take any chances walking through the kitchen door, just in case she'd let someone borrow her car, or she was trying to trick me by making me think she wasn't home.

I had Malia drop me off behind the house. "Thanks for everything, Malia," I said as I opened the car door. "I don't know what I'd do without you and Bridget."

"I hate that Bridget didn't come tonight," Malia said. "But honestly, I think this stuff would freak her out. She probably wouldn't be very open to the possibility of vampires. Hey, I meant to ask, what happened to your hand?"

I looked down at my closed fist but didn't remove the paper towel or look at the damage. I tend to heal at an extraordinarily fast rate and really didn't have a clue if I had a mark on me or if my palm was back to normal. No matter how "open" people claim to be about the paranormal, seeing it happen in real life tends to be a little overwhelming.

"Oh, nothing. I just cut it. It'll be fine."

"Well, I'll see you after school tomorrow."

"Take it easy. And thanks again."

She drove away, and I tiptoed through our backyard to the living room window. There was another window box planted with the same herbs that were in my own room. I plucked a bit of sage as I snuck a peek inside to see the twins and Oz playing Xbox and Rayden sitting on the couch reading. Aunt Doreen was bent over the coffee table, fussing over a tray of cookies. She straightened and turned to look directly at me. With a smile, she waved me to the kitchen.

How on earth did the woman do that? I swear the woman has eyes on every side of her head.

I turned back toward the driveway, and had to stifle a scream when I nearly walked smack into Noah.

Chapter 17

I jumped back, but I guess I didn't need to because he stepped away from me, as if he was repelled.

"Wha-what do you want with me?" I sputtered. I took another step toward him, and again he took another step back.

He looked the same, only paler. His eyes were no longer those beautiful warm, blue pools. They were icy and hard and red-rimmed.

"Do you like what you've done to me?" he hissed.

"I didn't do anything."

"Didn't you?" He reached out and grabbed my wrist but jerked his hand away with a yelp, then disappeared. So I hadn't dreamed up the disappearing act the first time.

Great.

Not only was he dichampyr, and stalking me, but he also could evaporate into thin air.

I hurried around the house, but Noah appeared again before I could reach the carport. He sneered at me and bared his fangs. "I can't wait to bury my fangs into that hot little neck of yours. We have unfinished business."

"Why aren't you doing it now, if you're so eager?"

"It's not time," he said. "Soon, though."

"If I did this to you, then you have to obey me. Sit!" I commanded.

He hissed.

"Too complicated a command? Let's try this one—play dead." I laughed. "Good boy."

His lips peeled back in a snarl. "Go ahead, laugh now."

"So if *I'm* not your master, who is?" I asked, trying to keep my composure. My hands were shaking and my heart was racing, like I'd just had a double shot of espresso for the first time. "It must be hard having no control over your own actions."

He just sneered. "I can't wait to taste you." I stepped forward and he shrieked and disappeared. Again.

"Hide-and-seek is for kids, Noah," I called.

His growling laughter echoed around me. My skin tingled, and the air pressure seemed to drop. I couldn't move. It was like a magnet pulled at my feet, preventing me from making my escape.

Aunt Doreen stepped outside. "Ariel, dearie. Is that you?" The moment she spoke, the magnet seemed to disengage.

I ran through the carport, past Aunt Doreen.

"There ye are," she said with a warm smile. "Yer mum was called into emergency surgery tonight, so she isn't here yet. Which is to yer benefit, aye?" She winked.

"How—?"

"When ye've lived this long and ye've raised as many wee ones as me, then ye learn a thing or two about their mischievous behaviors. Now come in, eat, and get to yer room before Mum punishes us both."

Aunt Doreen fixed me a heaping plate of fried chicken, roasted potatoes, and spinach salad while I went to the bathroom to wash my hands, check out the damage to my palm, and calm the fear racing through my veins.

What had stopped Noah from attacking me? He had reached for me, but it was like something invisible was keeping him at a distance. But what?

My wound had mostly healed. But there was a fresh

pink scar, which was unusual because I never scarred. *Ever.* I healed and the wounds just went away. That's how it has always been. But this time, I had a mark.

Not just any mark, either—it was in the shape of a backward S, like my birthmark. Except this one had a thin forked tongue at the tip of the S.

It was like the scrolls had branded me. What did this mean? Could they track me? Watch me? Hear me?

Dread seized my belly. Whatever it meant, I didn't like it.

I opened the medicine cabinet and pulled out the emergency kit. I placed a small square of cotton in my palm and wrapped the white medical bandage around my hand. I couldn't risk having someone notice I had a snake on my palm.

Seriously. If I were planning to get a tattoo, it would not have been a snake and it definitely wouldn't have been on my palm.

After I inhaled my dinner, I headed up to my room to shower and then hide from my mother.

No matter how good at this lying thing I was becoming, I still had a hard time keeping the truth from Momma. But I couldn't tell her. If I did, Mom would probably chain me to my bed and never let me leave again. Which might keep *me* safe, but it would definitely put the rest of the family at risk. And I know Noah wasn't bluffing. He'd left me the ribbon to prove it.

This was totally not cool.

I entered my room and smiled when I heard my stereo blaring the verse "I don't like your girlfriend." I hoped Ryan heard it. Sure, it was passive aggressive, but whatever. Who was I to care? He chased Lindsey after he kissed me. And not just any kiss, either. He made me knock-kneed.

And to make a girl loopy with your tongue and then run after another one was just not okay.

Spike was curled up on my pillow, and he purred extra loudly for me when I scratched his head. My cell phone rang, so I picked up the remote for my stereo and muted the volume, then answered.

"Hey. We missed you tonight," I said.

Bridget laughed. "Did y'all have fun getting your geek on with Mr. Green Eyes?"

"It was—interesting," I said.

"Oh? That sounds like it has juice potential. Spill."

Okay, so here I was at another one of those life-altering forks in the road. Bridget had been my best friend since forever, basically. She knew everything there was about me to know, except for the whole "vampire" thing. I wanted so bad to tell her everything. I knew I couldn't tell her about Noah, but maybe this stuff with the scrolls would be okay. She loved me enough to believe in me, right? I mean, Mr. Charles believed me, and he didn't even know me.

"Mr. Charles had the scrolls that Jill had shown us the other day."

"Boy, so far this isn't a yawner at all," she commented.

"Shut up and let me finish, cow!"

"Moo."

"He had the scrolls laid out and the one I had touched before still had the writing on it that had appeared after I touched it."

"Oh yeah, I'd forgotten about the magical AJ ink."

"Anyway, he asked me to tell him about what happened to me when I touched the scroll before, so I did."

"And he believed all that woo-woo about voices and reappearing ink?" she asked. My heart sank a little. Woo-woo was not the reaction I had been hoping for.

"He didn't act like it was crazy. But he wanted to test it out again."

"Mr. Charles wanted you to touch it and see for himself that you were making all that crap up in your head."

"Do you wanna hear this or not?" I asked, getting a little frustrated.

"Yeah, sorry. You know I want to hear it."

"Like I was saying, he wanted to test it out so he asked me to touch the seal of the second scroll like I did the first one. So I did. And it got really weird again. There were voices, and the seal burned me and, um, drew blood."

"And Mr. Charles heard the voices?"

"No. But when he pulled my palm off the seal, that's when it cut me."

"Hm," Bridget said.

"Hm. What?"

"It just seems odd that you're the only one hearing the voices, that's all."

"Mr. Charles wonders if there might be some family connection somewhere in my past." There. I opened the door to the conversation. If Bridget was ready for this discussion, she'd step through the door. If not, she'd slam it shut.

"Family connection? As in, someone in your family might've been a vampire? You're a descendant of the undead? Your great-great-grandmother could've been the Queen of the Damned? Seriously?"

"Something like that, yeah. What? You don't think it's a possibility? Even a remote possibility?"

Bridget laughed. Giggled, actually. She was near howling and gasping for breath after a couple of seconds. She finally calmed herself and replied, "I'd believe in shape-shifting worms before I'd believe that vampires were real."

"Technically speaking, caterpillars are shape-shifting worms," I said with a hollow laugh. Boy, had I read her wrong.

"Um. Yeah. Thanks for splitting those hairs for me, Mistress of the Dark."

I sighed. "Whatever. I guess Malia was right. You're not willing to be open about this. Thank God I have one friend who is."

"AJ! That's not fair—I . . ."

"Good night, Bridget," I said, cutting her off. Tears knotted in my throat as I powered down my phone. I didn't want to be tempted to answer if she called me back. This had been the worst week ever and Bridget's rejection was the cherry on top of a shitty sundae.

I walked into my bathroom and turned my shower on as hot as it would go. I pulled the shade down, but I could still hear Noah's laughter in the wind as I stripped off my clothes and stepped under the water to cry until the shower ran cold.

Chapter 18

I wrapped myself inside my warm terry cloth robe and brushed the tangles out of my wet hair. The shower hadn't washed away the hurt, nor had it disguised the tear stains on my face. But I still felt a little better.

As better as any vampire could feel after having her BFF drive a stake through her heart.

Yeah, yeah, it was a proverbial stake and Bridget didn't do it on purpose, but still. It hurt like a bitch. I guess I'd always fooled myself into believing that I could share *all* my secrets with her. I guess I was wrong.

"AJ?" Momma said with a knock to the door. "May I come in for a minute?"

"It's your house," I answered.

"Nice attitude," she said, closing the door behind her. She was carrying a package wrapped in brown paper. "This was delivered to you today."

I took the package, but there was no return address. "Thanks," I said, ripping through the paper. "I don't remember ordering anything."

It was a book. By all appearances it was a very old book. I opened it and a note card fell out. "Oh, it's from Jill, the bookstore lady over in Yellow Pine. Cool."

"What kind of book is it?" Mom asked.

"Well, I'm trying to find out more about our family history, so I'm researching. I'm assuming the book has something to do with that mysterious prophecy you told me about."

"Ariel, I was serious when I said you need to be very careful with this research. We can't risk being discovered. There are some very bad guys out there."

Who was she trying to talk to about bad guys?

"Don't worry, Momma. I'm being careful. The only people who know what I'm researching are Jill, Mr. Charles, Malia, and Bridge—and they all think it's for my paper. And since Mr. Charles was the one who suggested I go with an occult theme, it was the perfect cover."

"Why are you doing this?"

"I dunno, *Mom*. Isn't the 'surprise, you're a descendant of an evil vampire clan' enough of a reason? It's bad enough that I'm worried I could've killed Noah, but then, thanks to Auntie Tave's vision, or lack thereof, it seems highly probable I did kill him. And you're not full-blooded Serpentine, so the only thing you can do is give me more answerless questions. And Dad, well, he's nowhere to be found, and I couldn't trust him, anyway. So, that leaves me with two options: Find Dad and ask him these questions and risk everyone's necks, or do some good old-fashioned research on my own."

"About Noah," Momma said, patting the bed beside her.

Uh-oh. I had to be really careful here. Mom couldn't find out Noah was a dichamp. Not yet. He was very clear that he couldn't touch me, but all bets were off when it came to my family. If I told Mom, I had no doubt he would suck them lifeless. I couldn't risk that.

I sat next to Mom and she put her arm around me. "We got the test results back today. It definitely was *not* Serpentine venom."

Relief crashed through me like a flash flood. I had tried not to dwell on the possibility that I had done that to

Noah, but honestly, when you're being stalked by the evil undead, it's kinda hard not to think about it.

"Are you sure?"

"Positive. Serpentine venom is a lot like a fingerprint. It contains certain markers that are unique to the vampire it belongs to. It's pretty much venomous DNA."

"But if I didn't kill Noah, what did?"

"Believe it or not—a snake. Actually, the venom in his system is extremely rare and hasn't been seen in this area for a very long time. They have experts combing the O'Reily farm looking for the snake."

I sighed. I knew for a fact that wasn't true. But God knows I couldn't tell Mom.

And I had to know about the prophecy; I had to try to understand what was in my history and how I was connected to these documents. After today's episode, there was no doubt I was connected somehow.

Who had done that to Noah and why was he after me? Why me?

"Mom, will you be mad at me if I don't stop my research?"

She smiled. It was warm, but touched with a little sadness. "Would you stop if I asked you to?"

"Honestly? No."

"I didn't think so. But please don't trust anyone. You need to be very discreet. It's way too important that we stay hidden."

"Yeah, we wouldn't want the Serpentines to discover our location or the PTA to discover our fangs."

She chuckled and kissed my forehead before she stood to leave. "AJ, we've tried to have a family dinner all week and have failed miserably. This has been a terrible week for everyone. So I need you to promise me you'll be here tomorrow night."

"I will. What time?"

"Seven."

"Done. Mom, can I have permission to work with Mr. Charles while I'm suspended from school? I promise I'll just go to his classroom and back home. He's got some ancient texts that he's helping me decipher for my thesis."

"Okay. But please, *please* be careful. Don't trust anyone."

Careful was my middle name.

"One more question," I said as she started to leave. "Is there any way possible that Noah could've been bitten by a non-Serpentine vampire? Could he have, you know, been turned?" Of course, I knew the answer to this, but I wanted to hear her theory.

"Honey, are you worried about that because his body is missing?" she asked.

I nodded.

"The evening news reported that the funeral home he was sent to is under investigation for cremating bodies when the family asked for closed casket services. Apparently they're running a scam where they cremate the bodies, sell them multi-thousand-dollar coffins and plots, but bury empty pine boxes. They make a mint off their deception."

"That's terrible!" *And convenient.*

"Bad people are everywhere, not just in the vampire world," she said.

Mom left, shutting the door behind her.

I was about to put on my pj's when there was another knock at my door. "Did you forget something, Mom?" I asked as I opened it.

Ryan stood there with sad, puppy-dog eyes.

"Go away." I tried to close the door, but he was way too quick with his foot.

"AJ, can we talk? Please?"

"No. We tried to talk earlier, but that turned into tongue 'rasslin'. And since that is *never* gonna happen again, we can't talk."

"I promise I'll keep my tongue to myself."

"I don't care where you keep your tongue," I lied. I totally cared. I wanted him to keep his tongue in my mouth and away from that soul-sucking void of a human he was currently "not really dating."

"Please, AJ?"

"What the hell do you have to say to me? I can't be near you, Ryan. I let my guard down with you. I trusted you and then you chased after *her*? Acting like our kiss was a mistake? So I'm stopping it before it gets started again. Sorry, but I can't be your friend right now. And I certainly can't watch you be with her."

"I just wanted to apologize. Again," he said. "I miss you so much, and today in the kitchen, well, I couldn't help myself."

"Well, I hate that for ya, but from now on, resistance is not an option; it's mandatory. Good night, Ryan."

I kicked his shin. He jerked his leg back with a yelp, and I closed and locked the door.

He was still there, on the other side. I could feel him. I leaned my cheek and my palm against the cool wood and closed my eyes and listened to him breathe. I allowed myself to imagine he was mirroring me, and then I felt him—his warmth, his heart—reach out through the solid door and flow into me.

In that moment, he wasn't my stepbrother—he was just the boy I loved.

Too bad that moment couldn't last forever.

Chapter 19

Dear AJ,

I thought you might find this book of significance
to your research. It's an old English interpretation
of the Serpentine Scrolls and something called the
Frieceadan Runes of Destiny. I think you'll find the
text very interesting. I had never heard of the Runes
before, but it seems they are intimately connected
with the Scrolls. The Guardians of the Runes were
eradicated two centuries ago by the Serpentines.
Anyway, read this. Maybe you'll find another path to
take for your paper.

Good luck,

Jill

She was right. It was totally interesting. So much so that I stayed up all night reading it.

According to the text, there was once a group of magical people known as Frieceadan Druids. The women were "Mother Earth." They were gardeners, cooks, midwives, and healers. They had a talent for potions; they could manipulate the elements and had the greenest thumbs in the world, and though they had some use of magic, they couldn't cast spells. That wasn't the case for the men in the clan. They had all the power (isn't that always the way?). They not only had the earthly and elemental abilities the women had, they also could cast spells, do incantations, and, according to the lore, some could see into the future. Crescent moon birthmarks signified their magical status and no Frieceadan woman had ever been born with the mark. (What is it with birthmarks and paranormal beings, anyway?)

It was the "seeing into the future" part that got them into trouble. At one time, the Serpentines were allied with the Frieceadans, but it wasn't long before a small group of Serpentines began to make noise about tainted blood and losing power to the warlocks. This was all because one of the Frieceadan seers predicted the birth of a mixed-blood child whose blood would be the anti-serum for the

Serpentine venom. This child would bear the mark of both clans and its blood would effectively render the Serpentines powerless.

The seer inscribed his predictions into what is now known as the Serpentine Scrolls and the Runes of Destiny. I guess he was the warlock version of Nostradamus.

But the druids had very firm laws against recording their predictions in writing. It was considered an unhallowed practice, so it was strictly forbidden. So once the prophecy passed from oral to written, many in the Serpentine clan became fearful. A small, noisy group ousted the leaders and created their own laws.

In order to protect the prediction, and ultimately their destinies, the leaders of both races formed a high council and placed the runes under the protection of the Frieceadans, and the scrolls with the Serpentines.

The new clan elders did everything in their power to prevent the birth of this prophesied child, which meant not only killing off all the Frieceadan Warlocks but eliminating those who tried to leave the clan. And if anyone bearing the mark of the Serpentine couldn't be brought into the folds of the clan, they would meet a fate worse than death: They would be turned.

It almost made me understand why Dad went back

to them. I shuddered.

Being bitten by another vamp was the absolute worst punishment a genetically born vampire could face. It basically drains you of your human side, turning you into a dichampyr. Once turned, you're under the command of your creator until you become strong enough to release yourself or he deems you worthy of freedom. But there's nothing freeing about living a dichamp's powerless and feral existence.

The fact that the Serpentines would do this to their own kind told me more than I ever wanted to know about my family tree.

This family history of mine was not looking so swell. These were not stories I would want to tell my grandkids one day. "Don't worry, kids, we can't help that we're evil. We were just born that way."

The book went on to say that annihilating the Frieceadans to block the child prophecy actually worked *against* the Serpentines because the runes held a key to something greater than the prediction in the scrolls. When the elders learned this, they wanted the runes, but the secret hiding place had died with the last guardian. Seems the Serpentines had cut off their own nose to spite their face.

I rubbed my temples, trying to absorb all the information. A dull pain worked its way from my head down to my neck. I needed a massage. Preferably one given by a big, bulky dude name Sven with a penchant for necks.

Not biting them—rubbing them. Sheesh.

It was five A.M. and I hadn't slept a wink. I was totally amped up on caffeine, bloodsicles, and wicked family history. I lifted the shade to allow the sunrise to filter in. Noah was still out there. I'd felt him all night, though he never seemed to come near the house. He stayed on the perimeter of our property, prowling and sneering and generally trying to get into my head. Yet for once, I never felt unsafe, only uneasy.

I was dying to call Bridget, but since (a) it was too early to call anyone and (b) I wasn't talking to Bridget right now, there was no reason to.

But I had to talk to someone.

I decided to throw on a pair of shorts, a tank, and running shoes, grab my iPod, and hit the pavement until it was a decent hour. Then I'd call Malia.

I left a note in the kitchen in case Mom thought I was skipping out on my house arrest. All I was missing was an ankle bracelet. Hell, it probably wouldn't be too long before those things became part of a mandatory parenting kit.

This morning, I took the route I would've driven to school. I jogged past Bridget's house, which was still dark inside. All the while, Noah kept pace with me, sometimes running, sometimes jumping from tree to tree. His laughter echoed through my headphones, so I pumped up the volume and kept on running. I didn't know exactly why he was keeping his distance, but I had my suspicions that he wasn't allowed too close to me. Whoever had turned him controlled him. Noah was a youngling in the vampire world—he wasn't strong enough yet to break free.

He can't hurt you. They need you.

When the words popped into my head, I stopped short.

This voice was different. It wasn't like the voices in the scrolls—it felt safe, familiar in a way. And frankly, while I was being stalked by the undead, I would take any reassurance I could get. I figured if the voice was wrong and Noah broke away from his master, then I'd have to protect myself the old-fashioned way—fighting fang-to-fang.

Strangely, now that I knew Noah was not a product of my imagination or guilt, I wasn't nearly as frightened. Plus, my voice told me he couldn't hurt me. People always tell you to go with your gut, right?

Okay, maybe I was just being stupid. Whatever. He

was keeping his distance and that was really all that mattered.

At this hour, most houses were still dark, except for the few inhabited by old people who got up at four to read the paper and drink their first gallon of coffee.

As I ran, I pondered the new information that Jill had sent me. According to the book, the Serpentines were scared of losing their power. They had done everything they could to prevent the birth of the child whose blood would be their Kryptonite. But blocking the prophecy hadn't been enough. Now they needed the runes because they held the key to something bigger.

If all the Frieceadans had been eliminated, then how could the Serpentines find the runes? Were they actively searching for them and, if so, why *now*? I suppose it was possible that the Frieceadans hadn't been wiped out, but then wouldn't there be some mention of them somewhere? Surely there would at least be a rumor of their existence?

As I rounded the corner by the school, the sun peeked over the horizon and the sky began to fade to that unnamable shade of grayish purple. I kicked up my pace through the parking lot, down the alley behind the science building, and crossed over to Lake Drive, which would take me past Malia's house on my way back to mine. Maybe she'd be up and at it when I jogged by.

Or maybe not.

I sighed and slowed as I approached the lifeless house. I thought grandmothers were always up early. There goes my theory that the mandatory four A.M. rise time came automatically with your first grandchild.

Suddenly the air around me seemed to get lighter and I knew Noah was gone again. I was getting used to his angry and persistent presence, so it was quite noticeable when he wasn't around. It was like having a boulder lifted off my shoulders.

I stood on the small porch. Well, I could just knock on the door. It *was* six o'clock, and Malia would have to get up for school pretty soon, anyway. What difference would thirty minutes make?

I lightly rapped on the screen door. I don't know why I was so nervous. I guess it was probably because I hadn't seen Grandma Gervase since she took Malia away from us after her parents died. Grandma G. had always been a crotchety old woman; maybe knocking this early hadn't been such a great idea.

Just when I had talked myself into walking away, the door creaked open until the chain caught.

"Who's there?" an old woman barked.

"Um, Grandma Gervase? It's AJ Ashe, Malia's friend?"

"The roosters ain't up yet and you're knocking on my door? What's wrong with you, girl?"

"I'm sorry. I'll call Malia later."

"Never mind now," she said. "Damage is already done. I'll send her out."

I sat down on the stoop with my head in my hands. I had let my excitement over this Frieceadan stuff wash away any common sense I once owned.

The door opened behind me, but I didn't even want to turn and look. Malia carried out two cups of coffee, handed me one, and sat beside me.

"You're an idiot," she said with a laugh. "And what's that smell?" She sniffed and scooted away from me.

I took a drink. "Mmmm. God, I needed this." Then I sniffed my pits. "I don't smell that bad."

"Whatever. So what's going on? I'm assuming there's a reason you're here at this forsaken hour, risking life and limb in waking up the dead?"

"Oh, yeah. There's a reason. You won't believe what I discovered last night."

I told her everything (leaving out the detail that Noah isn't quite dead). As I delved deeper into the tale, her face changed from sleepy but tolerant to total fascination.

"AJ, you have to tell Mr. Charles!" she said.

"I will. I figured you could just give him an update at school today and then afterward we could meet."

"No way. We're telling him now." She jumped up and opened the door. "I'm gonna run in, change, and brush the funk from my mouth, then we're going to drive straight to Mr. Charles's place."

"Malia, we can't do that." I mean, technically, we could. Mr. Charles lived just a couple of blocks away. But still, just because we *could* didn't mean we *should*.

"Oh yes we can. This is important. I'll be right back. I'd invite you in, but given Grandma's current mood . . ." she said.

"Fine, I'll wait. But if he gets pissy with us, you're taking all the blame."

It was six-thirty when Malia pulled into Mr. Charles's driveway.

"This is not a good idea," I said for the umpteenth time.

"What are you afraid of?" Malia asked as she rang the doorbell.

"First of all, what if he had an overnight guest? We would be interrupting."

"Then we'd have some good gossip," she said.

"Malia, you're impossible."

Mr. Charles answered the door wearing a pair of running shorts and a short-sleeved Under Armour shirt. Yum.

"Ladies, what are you doing here? This is highly unusual. It had better be important."

"It's very important," Malia said. "AJ made a really cool discovery last night, Mr. Charles. Apparently the Serpentine Scrolls are somehow connected to the Fri—what were they called?" she asked, turning to me.

"The Frieceadan Runes of Destiny. I think in order to find out what I need to about the Serpentines, I need to start with the Frieceadan Warlocks."

Mr. Charles green eyes flashed bright. "This sounds very promising. Come on in."

After I told Mr. Charles the story, he picked up the phone and promptly called in sick.

"I can't possibly go in today. I would be way too distracted, anyway," he said.

"Then I'm skipping, too," Malia said.

"I don't think that's a good idea," Mr. Charles responded. "Your closest friend was suspended yesterday.

If you get caught skipping and you're with her, you could get into big trouble as well."

"So?"

"Malia, if you get caught ditching and hanging with me, not only will you get into trouble, but I'll get into *more* trouble," I said.

"But I don't want to miss out on any of the good stuff," she whined.

"Just go," I said, rolling my eyes. "I promise to fill you in on all the details when you get back this afternoon."

"Fine. I'll go, but I don't have to like it."

"Where is the book?" Mr. Charles asked.

"It's at home. Do you have the scrolls still, or did you return them to Jill?"

"I still have them."

"Why don't I run home, shower, grab the book, and meet you somewhere?"

"I need to be careful. I can't have people seeing me all over town, especially with a student, when I called in sick, you know."

"Why don't I just meet you at Jill's? She's bound to have more books in that house of hers. And nobody will be looking for you in Yellow Pine."

"Excellent idea, AJ. Okay, see you then."

After my shower, I set my alarm for eleven-thirty and promptly fell into a dark, dreamless sleep. I say dreamless but, really, that's not true.

It's like when you dream about the perfect guy, where you know him inside and out, like he was sewn together by a thread from your soul, but you never see his face. If you ever see that guy, you'll know him because he's a part of you. Then when you wake up, you question whether or not it really happened and if that guy really does exist.

Yeah, it was like that, only I didn't feel a connection to just one person. It was like being tied to a collection of souls.

I threw myself into a pair of jeans, my favorite Ramones T-shirt, and jeweled flip-flops. After I rewrapped my palm, I ran downstairs to clear the fog from my brain with a hemoshake and a side of toast.

Aunt Doreen came in carrying a large basket overflowing with a rainbow of vegetables, including the prettiest, fattest, reddest tomatoes I had ever seen. "There ye are, dearie. I'll fix ye a proper meal if ye'll give me a moment."

"Thanks, Aunt Doreen, but I'm about to head out. I'm working on a special project with one of my teachers."

"It must be a verra special project for your teacher to miss work."

"I think it is. We were researching one myth and we uncovered another. It's fascinating."

"I bet it is. Would that book have anythin' to do with yer research?" she asked, pointing to the book Jill had sent me.

"Yes, ma'am."

She dumped the basket into the sink and hung her wide-brimmed hat on the wall hook by the door. "Mind if I snitch a look?" she asked, taking the book from me. "Where's yer necklace? Grown tired of it already?" she asked.

"Oh, I forgot to put it back on after my shower." Aunt Doreen flipped the book open as I glanced at the clock on the wall. "Oh, shi—I mean, crap. I'm gonna be late! Sorry, Aunt D. Can I show this to you later?"

"Of course," she said, handing the book back. "Ariel, dear. Be careful digging up old bones. Sometimes they don't want to be uncovered."

I slid off my barstool and bent to kiss Aunt Doreen on the cheek. She was really growing on me. "I'll be careful. We're just researching myths for a paper."

"Sometimes there's a fair thin line betwixt fable and

fact, my dear. Old bones should rest in peace. Here," she said as she slipped a small herb bouquet into my bag. "I just love the way these keep everything smelling so fresh, don't you?"

I laughed. "Are you suggesting I'm stinky?"

"Maybe a wee bit."

Note to self: Switch deodorant.

Chapter 20

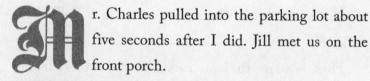r. Charles pulled into the parking lot about five seconds after I did. Jill met us on the front porch.

"Come on in!" she said, ushering us into the bookstore. "I've got the tables cleared off in the back, and you two can stay as long as you like."

"Thanks for letting us intrude, Jill," Mr. Charles said.

"Morris, friends are never an imposition. You know that."

I snickered. I couldn't help myself. "Seriously, Morris?"

"I told you, it's a very respectable name," Jill chastised me. "I'll bring y'all some tea and cookies in a little while.

If you need anything, Morris knows his way around."

"Thanks, Jill. You're the best," I said. "Now, where do we start?"

"This book is supposed to be a translation of the scrolls. It makes me wonder if there was ever a translation done of the runes," Mr. Charles said. He slid his messenger bag off his shoulder and pulled out his Mac PowerBook.

He pulled up Google and entered his search words. Great, only two million possible matches. No problem.

"Okay, why don't you weed through some of these hits and see if you can narrow the search a little. I'll start comparing the scrolls to the text and see how closely they translate."

He handed me the laptop and I started sifting through the pages and pages of website hits.

Four hours and one headache later, I finally pulled my eyes off the screen. "I think I've got something here," I said. I placed the laptop on the table.

Mr. Charles put down the book, took off his reading glasses, and rubbed his eyes. "Just in time. I need a change of pace."

"I found an obscure reference to the Frieceadans on a Wikipedia page that I followed to this site. Look at this."

Mr. Charles put his glasses back on and started to read.

"Many believe the Frieceadans were victims of the genocidal Serpentines, but in the book *The Bloody Truth* we discover there was more to the story. Trouble started when the Serpentines learned of the runes' hidden power."

"What do you think?" I asked.

"It's somewhere to start. It makes sense that the Serpentines would be after something powerful—especially if that power was somehow connected to the scrolls."

"Mr. Charles, this is all just mythology. You act like there are really vampires walking among us."

"That's because I believe there are. But people are so afraid of the monsters in the past that they can't see the humans they've become."

"I've just never met anyone who was so open-minded about this stuff."

He smiled and went back to reading. Mom's warning bounced around in my head, reminding me not to trust anyone with our secret. But it was so tempting. I had lived a lie my whole life, and here was someone who would be willing to listen and not judge me for being different.

I stood and stretched.

There are two paths to your fate. Which road will you travel down?

My knees buckled. Where was the voice coming from?

I had been trying very hard to deny my connection to the scrolls and anything with my Serpentine history. I lived so much in denial of my vampire side that I had almost convinced myself all this really was for a paper and not for me. The fact was, I knew I hadn't killed Noah now, so why was I so hell-bent on continuing this research?

Do not deny your destiny. Do not ignore your history. Embrace both parts of your soul.

"I know why the Serpentines are after the Runes of Destiny!" Mr. Charles suddenly exclaimed, showing me the screen. "Apparently they believe the runes control time. With all the runes in place, one could travel into the past to change the future. Imagine how different the world would be today if the runes fell into the wrong hands. The high council was formed to protect both the scrolls and the runes. Each member of the council became a key holder. Guardianship was passed down through the generations. Only those bearing the mark of a key holder would be granted access to the secrets of the runes and the scrolls."

Mr. Charles put the computer down and looked at

me with excitement-laced eyes. "Do you know what this means?" Mr. Charles asked.

"Not a clue."

"It means," he said with an exasperated sigh, "that if there is one shred of truth to this, then you, my friend, could be a key holder."

"Ha-ha. Very funny, Mr. Charles," I said, not thinking it funny at all.

"I've seen your reaction to the scrolls, AJ. There's not a doubt in my mind. You are linked to them—by blood."

"Fine. I've had a reaction. But how on earth does that make me a key holder?"

"The text says the key holders are drawn to and marked by the scrolls. I think you need to tell me the truth now, AJ."

"There's nothing to tell," I said, nervously playing with the bandage on my palm.

"I think there is." Mr. Charles stood, walked over to me, and took my bandaged hand in his. He gently pulled the tape off and, just before he pulled the cotton pad off to reveal my scar, I closed my fist.

"I'm thirsty. Want a Coke?" I turned to walk away, but he pulled me back.

"AJ, don't be frightened." He pushed my hair behind

my ear and smiled. "It's okay. You can tell me anything. I will not reject you. I promise."

Tears stung my eyes, but I refused to let them fall.

Be careful where you put your trust. What does your heart say?

Dammit! As much as my gut screamed to trust him, that voice kept telling me no. And I felt compelled to listen.

"I need to go home," I said. "I promised Mom I wouldn't be late for dinner, and it's already five o'clock."

Mr. Charles pulled me into a hug, which was just the incentive my tears needed to fall. Fine. I'm a big ol' titty-baby. Whatever.

"Whenever you're ready," he said, ending the hug and wiping my tears away with his thumb. "I'm here. Okay?"

"Okay."

"Let me talk to Jill real quick about this new information. I'm betting she can help us find this book. Then I'll take you home."

"No. That's okay. I can drive." My cell phone rang as I packed up. I left the scrolls on the table, refusing to touch them again, then walked to my car and answered.

"Hello," I said without looking at the caller ID.

"Hey. Can we talk?"

I sighed. It was Bridget.

"It's a free country. Talk away," I said.

"Will you promise you won't hang up?"

"I won't promise you anything."

"I'm so sorry, AJ. I saw Malia today and she told me you were really mad at me."

"I am." How did Malia know? I hadn't told her that.

"I didn't mean to hurt you."

"Well, you did. You laughed at me, and you're supposed to be my best friend. I've needed you all week and you've totally tossed me to the side for Grady."

"I know. But you're acting all weird and stuff. And I don't get what it is you need from me. Am I really supposed to believe you could hear voices coming to you from those scrolls?"

"Yes. You are. Because why would I lie about that?"

"I don't think you're lying, exactly."

"But you don't believe me. See, that's what I need from you, to believe me." I said.

This time she sighed. It was a heavy, sad sound and it told me all I needed to hear.

"I've gotta go, Bridge."

"AJ—" I heard her say as I clicked my phone shut, cutting her off.

My heart weighed a ton, and more tears welled up in a knot in my throat. I started the car, and to avoid having a pity party I got lost in thought on the drive home.

I had wanted to tell Mr. Charles everything, but at the risk of losing the only ally I really had right now, I couldn't open up. Mom's warning to be careful nagged at me. Right now, it had to be enough that Mr. Charles accepted I might have vampire lineage somewhere in my family. That was more than even my supposed BFF could do.

I really couldn't trust anyone because there was another vampire out there—and the product of his work was unbreathing down my neck. And using my family's safety to keep me in check. I had to be very careful. Probably taking that run this morning hadn't been such a great idea. Duh.

Of course, if I were to believe the information we found today, then the runes would be worth killing for. They could travel back in time to change the future. What a great way to ensure the fate of your clan. But according to the lore, you'd need one Frieceadan and one Serpentine key holder to access the location of the runes. And by all accounts, the Frieceadans had been wiped out.

By my ancestors.

Good God. I didn't know what to believe anymore. Hell, I know for a fact I'm a vampire, and I'm having a hard time believing *I'm* real.

I walked into the kitchen to find Oz and the twins digging through Ryan's backpack.

"What are y'all into now?" I asked.

"Nothing," they said in unison.

"Whatever it is, just stay away from my stuff, got it?"

They all nodded and went back to their snooping. I was walking through the kitchen toward the stairs when I overheard Ryan and Rayden whispering.

"You seriously haven't found it?" Rayden asked.

"Seriously. It's pissing me off, too," Ryan said. "I should have it because I have the, um, other stuff that goes with it."

"Have you looked everywhere? You know, maybe in a not so obvious place. Like where I found mine."

"Duh. Ya think? I've looked everywhere. And I do mean *everywhere*."

"I don't know what it is you're looking for, but if it's in your backpack, the twins will find it before you do," I said loudly as I walked up the stairs.

"Dammit!" Ryan yelled. "Oz, where did the girls go? They were just here!"

I laughed all the way to my room. Boy, that felt good.

I opened the door and jumped when I saw Malia sitting on my bed. "You scared the crap outta me. I didn't know you were here. Where's your car?"

"I felt like taking a walk and the twins let me in. So, tell me what happened today."

"I'll do you one better—I'll show ya."

I grabbed my laptop off my bedside table and noticed the window box had fallen to the ground. "Aw. My pretty new window box must've come loose. Gotta remember to tell Aunt Doreen." Sitting on the bed next to Malia, I pulled up the website Mr. Charles and I had found.

"Time travel? Really?" Malia asked skeptically while reading the website.

"It seems the Serpentines thought so. Not sure what I believe. But I guess all that matters is what they believed and what they were willing to do to find the runes."

"I talked to Bridget today. She seems really upset," Malia said.

"Yeah. She's upset, but not enough to believe me."

"You don't need friends like that."

My heart sank with that statement. "I miss us. We were three peas in a pod."

"Sometimes people change." Malia's cell phone

beeped. She pulled it off her hip and flipped it open to read the message.

Her mouth dropped open. "No way."

"What?" I asked.

"Go to your Facebook page," Malia said.

"Okay, but why? I haven't been there all week."

I typed in the address and nearly passed out when my site came up. New pictures of me and Mr. Charles had been uploaded to my profile. Lots of them. Pics of us hugging, of him touching my face, of my head on his shoulder. Most of them were from today, but some looked like they had been poorly Photoshopped. There was even a picture that looked like we were kissing.

"We didn't . . . I don't . . . Who? Why?" I couldn't speak because there wasn't a coherent thought in my brain.

"I don't know, but this isn't good. Crap. If I'm getting a text, then that means everyone has seen it by now."

The house phone and my cell phone rang simultaneously, and for about the hundredth time this week all hell seemed to break loose in my world.

Chapter 21

"Hello," I answered tentatively when I didn't recognize the phone number on my display.

"AJ, this is Sheriff Christopher. I need to ask you a few questions. Are you at home right now, darlin'?"

"Um, no," I lied.

"Well, I'm sittin' here in your kitchen and that sweet little Aunt Doreen says she thought you were right upstairs."

"Um, I haven't seen Aunt Doreen since this morning." I shot Malia a "help me" look.

"What?" she mouthed silently.

I put my hand over the receiver and whispered, "Sheriff."

"Shit," she said.

No shit.

"I've got time to wait. Your momma is on her way home, too. Seein' as how you don't like to answer any questions without her present and all."

Oh, God. This was not going to end well.

"Okay, Sheriff. I'll be there in just a few minutes. Thanks for calling." I clicked my phone shut and looked up to see Ryan standing in the doorway.

"Is it true?" he asked. "Are those pictures true?"

"Close the door," I hissed. "Hurry. The sheriff is downstairs looking for me and I can't face him until I know what the hell is going on. And no, those pictures aren't true."

"But they're on your account?" Ryan said, the pain in his voice causing my heart to skip a beat.

"I know. But I'm being set up. Why would I post those pictures on my account? How stupid do people think I am? I swear. Besides, Mr. Charles is hot and all, but he's got to be in his *thirties*! And he's a teacher!"

Malia cleared her throat. "We've got to get AJ out of here. Can you help us?"

"Yeah. I have to talk to the sheriff, anyway. He's probably here to question you about Noah again. I'm going to tell him the truth, AJ. He knows we've been covering for each other and he's just trying to get one of us to admit it."

"What will happen to you?" I asked.

"It doesn't matter. I didn't kill Noah. I just hit him in the face a couple of times, and when I left he was still standing. I know I should've told them I hit Noah before now, but I was scared. And then when you covered for me, I didn't know what to do."

I hugged Ryan and whispered, "It's my turn to apologize. I'm so sorry for everything."

He smiled, but his eyes were sad. "I would do anything for you," he said.

"Okay, great. Can we move on from this tragic love story to the now? How do we get AJ out of here?" Malia said.

"The old-fashioned way," Ryan answered. "My window."

Ryan's room was across the hall from mine. One of his windows opened to a flat section of roofing that led right to a large, sturdy tree branch. Which was attached to a giant tree trunk with little pieces of wood nailed to it like a ladder.

"I had started building us a new tree house but never

quite finished," Ryan said.

It was the perfect escape route.

"Dammit. I should've changed shoes!" I said as I slid onto the limb and my pretty little sandal flopped onto the ground.

"No time to worry about that now," Malia said. "Just keep shimmying."

I managed to make it to the ground with no splinters, no broken bones . . . and no plan.

"You walked here, so we don't have your car. And my keys are in my bag, which is in my room. Now what?" I asked, slipping back into my shoes.

"Here!" Ryan whisper-yelled from the window. "Take my Jeep. I parked it in the alley behind the house." He tossed me his keys.

"Um, I don't drive a stick," I said.

"I do. Let's go," Malia grabbed the keys from me and we took off for the alley.

"I don't even know why we're running," I said as Malia started the Jeep and ground it into gear.

"Because you need to get some answers before you face the police. Or your mother. We're going to see Mr. Charles."

"Is that smart? I mean, there are pictures of us on the

internet. Fake pictures, but still. We need to figure out who the hell posted those," I said. Could this week get any worse?

My phone rang again. It was Mom.

"Where are you?" she yelled.

"Why?" I asked.

"Because I have some questions for you, Ariel, that's why. The sheriff just took Ryan down to the station because he admitted to beating Noah up. Then Octavia called in a panic saying I had to find you because something didn't feel right—that you've been keeping secrets. So I ran home and Doreen said you were upstairs, but the only thing I found in your room was your laptop. And imagine my surprise when I saw those pictures. Octavia was right again—you've been keeping secrets."

"Mom. Those pictures are fake. I don't know who did it, but I'm going to find out. I've been set up. I swear."

"Honey, that's all you've been saying lately—and frankly, I'm starting to think I can't trust a word that comes out of your mouth. It's been nothing but secrets and lies—I think it's time you start taking a little responsibility for your actions," she said. "And if Mr. Charles took advantage of you, we have to know. You can't keep covering for the people you care about."

"When have I ever lied to you?"

"You lied to protect Ryan. You're lying now! Honestly, it seems you've lost all contact with the truth, Ariel."

"Mom. That's not fair. I wanted to protect Ryan because I know he didn't kill Noah. And that was wrong. But I haven't lied to you about anything else. Not the test *or* Mr. Charles. You know I'm telling you the truth." Okay, technically, withholding the truth about Noah being a vampire wasn't a lie, it was an omission.

"I don't know any such thing, but if you'll come home, I promise I'll give you the benefit of the doubt," she said.

I wished I could believe her. "I'll be home in a little while," I said.

I ended the call and realized I had received about a dozen text messages, most from other girls congratulating me for doing Mr. Charles. Seriously? People were so stupid.

And then there was a 911 text from Bridget. The thought of hearing her tell me she didn't believe me was too much, so I shut my phone off. I couldn't handle any more drama.

Malia drove through the neighborhood and turned onto Mr. Charles's street. His car wasn't in the carport and the house was dark.

"Well, he's not home," I said.

"We could stop anyway and wait for him," she suggested.

"Maybe I should just go home."

"We need to find out who posted those photos. There's one person I can think of who hates you this much—Lindsey. I say we confront her."

Ugh. The very idea of talking to Lindsey Rockport was enough to give me the hives. But Malia was right. In a warped way, Lindsey was the only person who had anything to gain from this.

But I couldn't believe for a second that Lindsey would stoop this low. She was a bitch, but was she a wack job? Would she really do this to Mr. Charles and me? Would she ruin the lives of two people just to get back at me? In my mind, she was already the clear winner. She had Ryan and she would probably be president. Was she so pissed off that she would risk everything just to see me humiliated?

We drove through the square to the other side of town. Lindsey's house backed up to the city park. It was in a prime location, but the house itself was in need of some major TLC. The paint was peeling, one of the shutters was missing, the gutters were overflowing with pine needles, and the yard really needed a lawn boy.

We parked on the street next to the mailbox and walked to the front porch. I took a look inside the screen door to see Bridget and Lindsey huddled on the floor with a laptop positioned between them.

"Are you freaking kidding me?" I yelled, opening the screen, making them jump. "Bridge, I knew you were mad at me, but really? How could you?"

She couldn't have looked guiltier if she'd tried.

"AJ, it's not what you think," Bridget said.

"Isn't it?" I asked. "We came over to find out if Lindsey was the one who hacked my Facebook account. It never occurred to me you would've been behind it. Are you that pissed off at me?"

Lindsey stood up and came to Bridget's defense. "Hold on a minute. I'm certainly not your biggest fan, but Bridget is. She came over here and tore me a new one because, like you, she assumed I had something to do with this. I didn't even know what she was talking about," Lindsey said.

I looked at Bridget and she nodded. "I wanted to kill whoever had done this to you. I was convinced it was Lindsey. Now I'm wondering if maybe it was Ryan?"

"No, it wasn't. I saw him a few minutes ago and he was as shocked as me." I collapsed next to Bridget on the floor and put my head on her shoulder. "I'm sorry, Bridge.

This has been the worst week and I haven't been thinking straight since Noah died. What am I gonna do now?"

Bridget wrapped an arm around my shoulders. "You mean, what are *we* gonna do now?"

God, it felt good to have my friend back.

Chapter 22

Malia was off making a phone call and Bridget was in the kitchen grabbing everyone a Coke. Lindsey and I were sitting alone in her living room staring at her laptop, with only my occasional sniffling to break the thick silence.

"I'm, uh, sorry I was such a bitch," Lindsey said.

I smiled as best I could. "You weren't the only one being a bitch. I'm sorry, too," I said. There, that felt a little better.

"I was jealous of you and Ryan. As much fun as we have together, he's totally in love with you. But I guess I'm just hoping that after some time passes, I won't only be his runner-up girl."

"This whole situation sucks. And ironically, having

major non-brotherly feelings toward my stepbrother isn't the worst thing that's happened to me this week."

I glanced around the room noting the peeling paint, the cracks in the wall, and the layer of dust lining all the flat surfaces. "Where do your parents work?" I asked.

"It's just me and my dad, and he works two jobs, so he's not really home very much."

"Oh." I suddenly felt very ashamed. I had everything—a warm home filled with friends and family. Lindsey wasn't lackluster, she was just lonely.

Bridget walked into the room carrying three cans of Coke and sat them on the coffee table. Her face was pale, and there was a worry line between her eyebrows.

"What?" I asked her.

"It's nothing. I guess I'm probably just overreacting to something I thought I heard Malia say on the phone."

"What do you mean?" I asked. I glanced through the kitchen to see Malia standing on the back deck, still talking into her cell.

"It was weird. She said 'grandma' a couple of times really loudly, but then she started to whisper. I dunno. It just struck me as odd."

"Her grandmother has been calling a lot lately. She's probably just getting tired of being micromanaged. I feel really bad that I haven't even talked to her about why her grandmother has been calling so much. I've been so focused on me. And Malia has been a trooper. She's been one of the few people I could depend on this week."

Bridget's face fell.

"I'm sorry. I honestly didn't mean that as a slight against you. I'm just trying to point out that she has no motive to hurt me like this."

"I know. But my gut is telling me something's off."

"What's off?" Malia asked from the doorway.

"Oh. You're off the phone. Was that your grandmother?" I asked.

"Yeah. She's always checking in on me. Especially when she goes to the coast to see Aunt Myrtle."

"You have the house to yourself for the weekend? That could be fun," Lindsey said.

"It could be if I had someone to have fun with. Anyway, what were you saying wasn't right?" she asked, turning to look at me.

"Bridget and I were just talking about Ryan being taken to the police station even though he obviously didn't kill Noah. And how Mr. Charles will be in trouble, but only because we're being framed," I lied. "That's it! I know what I need to do now."

"What?" they all three asked together.

"Running was stupid. The longer I stay away, the guiltier I look. Maybe I should just go to the police station and straighten this whole mess out."

"Why would you want to go there?" Malia asked. "It's obvious they won't believe anything you say, so you'll be wasting your time. And hell, with your luck, they'll probably just arrest you."

"I'll take my chances. Now, who's gonna drive me?"

"I'll go if you guys don't care. I don't have a car, though," Lindsey said.

"Me too. But I don't have a car either. I walked here," Bridget said.

We all turned to look at Malia. She made a big production of rolling her eyes and sighing dramatically before saying, "Fine. I'm in, too. But I'm not stepping foot inside that station. Cops give me the heebies."

"Cody Littleton didn't give you the heebies when you were in eighth grade," I reminded Malia as we walked out to the Jeep.

"Ew. I had forgotten about that. Don't remind me."

"What was it you called him?" Bridget asked. "Cow tongue?"

"No, it was camel tongue," I said.

We loaded ourselves into the Jeep and Malia drove us the fifteen blocks or so to the police station. As we were pulling into the parking lot, Malia's phone rang.

"Hello?" she said.

After a few seconds she turned to me and asked, "Do you have your phone on?"

"No. I turned it off. I was getting congratulations spam from all the idiot girls in town."

"Mr. Charles is at home and he needs to talk to you," Malia said.

Bridget kicked my chair from behind. "AJ, no. That is a bad idea," she said.

"Shut up, Bridget. Have you forgotten that AJ isn't the only victim here?" Malia asked.

"No. I haven't. But wouldn't it look bad if AJ and Mr. Charles are caught together?" Bridget countered.

"Wouldn't it be smarter if they went to the police together? There's strength in numbers," Malia said, turning to face me. "It's up to you, AJ. I'll support whatever decision you make. Ultimately, your life is the only one that will be affected by this decision, anyway."

A knot had formed in my belly that had to be the size of a grapefruit. I needed the 911 girl inside me to kick in and tell me what to do.

Let your quest for the truth help you choose your path. Whatever choice you make, tread carefully.

A sense of relief filled me. I took a deep breath and said, "I'm really not ready to face the sheriff yet. Take me to Mr. Charles. Malia's right—it would be best if he and I show a united front and go to the police together." All right. And when all this was over, that guiding light of mine was going to have to quiet down. I was starting to feel a little schizoid.

"Then I'm going with you," Bridget said. "Something's not right here, and you need a friend."

"Actually, will you go to the station and find Ryan? I need to know he's okay. Please?"

The Valley Springs, Mississippi, police station was housed in a nondescript metal building just across the street from Rudy's—the best burger joint in the tri-county region. Rudy also happened to be the only bail bondsman in the tri-county region. You could drive through, post your bond, and grab a burger to go.

Malia parked near the front entrance and Bridget and Lindsey got out.

"We'll catch a ride home," Bridget said.

"What if Mr. Charles has already been arrested?" I asked.

"He hasn't been," Malia said. "I mean, would he have asked us to meet him at his house if he were sitting in jail? Besides, they can't arrest him until they've at least questioned you. Right? And do they even count seventeen as underage in Mississippi?" She laughed.

"Ha-ha. They do if it's with a teacher," I said. "Okay, Bridge, find Ryan for me."

"Will do," Bridget said. "Be careful. And don't go in by yourself. Okay?"

"Okay."

Malia took a left out of the parking lot and headed toward Mr. Charles's house.

"I really resent that she thinks I'm being a bad friend," Malia said.

"She doesn't think that," I said. "She's just worried about me."

"Whatever. She's treated me like the redheaded stepchild since I returned. I think she wishes Katrina would've swallowed me up along with our house."

"That's not true. It's been the two of us since ninth grade. And this week has been an anomaly. Once all this is over, we'll find our groove again."

Malia parked on the street in front of Mr. Charles's house and we walked to the door together. His car still wasn't in the carport.

"He's not here," I said.

"He told me he'd meet us here. He said the door was unlocked and to go on in."

My self-preservation alarm kicked in and I hesitated as Malia opened the door. "Um, I've changed my mind."

"What?" Malia asked.

"I dunno. Doesn't this feel weird to you?"

"This whole damn week has been weird, AJ. Noah's dead, you've been suspended, and there are pictures of you and Mr. Charles on Facebook. This is the least weird thing that's happened all week."

Fair enough.

"Maybe we should wait outside for him," I suggested.

"Yeah, that wouldn't be weird at all. What if someone drove by and saw you sitting on his front porch waiting? You know what they would assume, right? Just go on in. Mr. Charles said he wouldn't be long."

She had a point. I couldn't sit outside and wait for him. And honestly, what was I worried about? Mr. Charles was a victim just like me. We needed a game plan. We needed to figure out who had done this to us, and then we needed to go to the police . . . together.

Malia's phone began to ring as I stepped into the

house. "Jesus, Grandma. What now?" Malia said, looking at the caller ID. "Hello? Yeah. What? Oh my God! I'm leaving now." Malia clicked her phone shut, her face stricken. "Grandma fell down the stairs and broke her hip. She's in the hospital in Ocean Springs. I've got to go."

"Oh, Malia! I'm so sorry. Of course you have to go—I'll be fine here," I said, pulling her into a hug. "Be careful, though. Don't get yourself into an accident rushing to her side."

"Aren't you coming with? I have to take Ryan's Jeep back anyway," she asked, quickly pulling out of the hug.

"No, I'll stay. Everything's cool. You go."

Malia squeezed my hand. "I'm sorry." Then she ran back to the Jeep and drove off like a bat out of hell.

I entered the house, closing the door behind me. It was dark and quiet.

"Mr. Charles?" I called, just in case he was home. There was no answer, but there was a noise in the back of the house.

I walked through the small living room into the hallway and flipped on the light. "Mr. Charles? Are you here?"

The silence was broken by the sound of a *thwack* coming from one of the bedrooms.

Slowly I walked down the hall. Okay, I know this was a sci-fi horror flick moment and I was being the girl who walked down into the dark basement all alone. But hell, I'm a vampire. They should fear *me*, right?

"Hello?"

I reached the first bedroom on the right, flipped the light switch, and a giant calico cat nearly knocked me over as it ran out of the room.

I shrieked. "You scared me, cat!"

"Meow," it said, obviously bored with me already.

The room was clearly a home office. There were loaded bookshelves lining the walls; a Mac and several file folders called the desk home; and a table in the center of the room was covered in loose-leaf paper and photos.

There was a book open on the floor, next to the desk. I walked into the room, bent down to pick it up, and realized it was a journal.

Mr. Charles's journal.

Okay, I know I shouldn't read it. Honestly, there is almost nothing worse than that kind of violation, but I couldn't help myself.

The last entry was dated yesterday.

Plan is in place. AJ has been suspended and feels alone. I am gaining her trust.

What!?

My heart hammered in my throat. I flipped backward in the book to the previous entry.

I suspect AJ might be a Serpentine descendant. She hasn't shown me physical evidence yet, but I believe with some persuasion I can get her to open up. She is my key to becoming immortal.

I flipped through to the beginning, where Mr. Charles outlined how he was going to gain my trust.

Master led me here to find the chosen one. I have studied all students for a year and have found one prospect that I believe could be the one.

Have decided I need to leave bread crumbs to see if she responds.

I. Leave AJ note asking her to work with me on thesis.

II. Alienate AJ from friends and family: Must get AJ suspended from school in order to work with her alone. Cheating on test? Yes! How? Test key? Copying? Both?

My hands started shaking as I read on.

III. Continue to gain her trust. Make her feel safe with me so I can take her willingly to the elders. Much easier if she is willing.

My stomach turned. I tossed the book down, and it nudged the mouse, bringing the computer back from sleep. And let me just say, I had no idea what panic was until I saw the Photoshop program on-screen, with the freshly doctored pictures of Mr. Charles and me.

I had to swallow my bile. I turned to run away. And ran right into Mr. Charles instead.

Chapter 23

"Um," I said, stumbling backward. "Hi, Mr. Charles." Stay strong, AJ. Think.

"AJ, I think you can probably call me Morris now, don't you?"

He smiled, but his eyes weren't as warm as usual. They were kinda bugging out with excitement. He seemed a little tweaked, like a junkie looking for a fix, and that had me freaking out a bit.

"Bridget is on her way to pick me up. I told her I'd be waiting outside."

His smile deepened. "That's not true, AJ. I just saw Bridget on the square a few minutes ago with Lindsey." He stepped into the room. "I don't want you to be frightened of me. I'm the one person you can be yourself around."

Fear gripped me and my head began to swim. I grappled in my purse for my phone, but Mr. Charles was too quick. In one motion he knocked my bag away and pulled my arm behind my back.

"I know this is a shock to you," he said in a hushed voice. "But I think if you'll examine the situation, you'll see that fate brought us together."

His breath was hot on my neck as he pulled my hair away. He traced my birthmark and sighed. "I knew it! This is my proof. The clan elders have been waiting for you."

"Proof of what? What clan elders? Dude, you need to put down the crack pipe," I said, grasping to keep my charade going. But there was no fooling him. He knew.

He had always known.

"AJ, you can stop the facade now. It's time to meet your destiny. The leaders of your clan sent me here to find you and bring you back. Once I bring you to them, they'll turn me. I'll finally be immortal."

"You really are high. You seriously can't believe you'll be immortal? Surely you know that, being an occult expert and all. If they've promised you immortality, they were yanking your chain," I said, finally giving up the act.

He laughed. It was deep and gravelly and I felt it

almost as much as I heard it.

"I know you're scared, but honestly, they won't hurt you. They need you alive." He grabbed my burned hand and pulled off the bandage. "You're the key holder, just like they suspected. They can't get to the runes without you."

"Are you forgetting that the Frieceadans hid the runes and the Serpentines killed the Warlocks off before they found out where the runes were located?"

"You let me worry about that. We need to leave. I almost screwed things up with that Facebook page. I programmed the wrong damned date. We were supposed to be gone before the pictures hit the web. Now we have to hurry."

I felt something cold and hard pressed against my back. "This is just my little insurance policy that you'll cooperate. We're going out the back door."

"I'm confused," I said as he nudged me out of the bedroom with the gun. "How did the clan elders know about me?"

"Well, your father, of course."

My father? Rage pushed through my veins, flashing red behind my eyes. My senses sharpened so quickly, my head buzzed and the floor seemed to swirl beneath my feet. Mr. Charles's grip tightened, and he poked the barrel of the gun deeper into my kidney.

The voice spoke to me again.

Set your instincts free and let them guide you.

Suddenly I knew why the voice was familiar. It was Octavia.

You can do this.

With her words something inside me snapped. Like a choreographed dance move, I popped my shoulder down and jabbed him with my elbow, causing him to lose balance and stumble backward. Then I wrenched my arm free and knocked the gun from his grip. And I ran like hell.

I was fast, but not fast enough. Why hadn't I worked on honing my super speed? Why had I been so determined to forget my vampire side that I hadn't worked on any of my super skills?

I reached the kitchen only to be tackled before I could get to the door. "I really wish you hadn't done that, AJ," Mr. Charles said. "Now I'm going to have to medicate you."

I felt a pinprick in my arm and the red behind my eyes flashed bright, my fangs descended, and I seemed to levitate from the ground, tossing Mr. Charles to the side. I floated above him for a nanosecond, and his eyes widened with excitement. And so did mine.

Holy shit! I never would've denied I was a vampire if I had known I could fly!

The rush was amazing but short-lived.

I wish I could say that I flew away to safety, but obviously I need to work on my flying skills because I fell. And as luck would have it, I landed right on top of Mr. Charles.

My head was spinning, my stomach was churning, and I could feel my fangs receding. What the hell was that about? Usually I couldn't make my fangs recede to save my life, but when I needed them most, they disappear?

Mr. Charles chuckled as he readied the syringe and wrapped his arms back around me. "Okay, let's try this one more time—"

I sensed a movement behind me as strong hands wrenched me free of Mr. Charles's arms.

"What the—?" Mr. Charles shouted in surprise as the syringe flew free.

For a brief moment, I thought I was being rescued. Then I saw the red eyes of my savior and realized that Noah James was not done with me.

"She's mine," he hissed at Mr. Charles.

"You haven't been released, Noah. You can't have her until after the clan uses her," Mr. Charles said, all too knowingly.

"Her wall of protection is gone. I released myself," he spat.

My wall of protection?

Noah turned to me. "Do you know my favorite part of being a vampire?" he asked.

"No clue," I said, realizing this was not going to end well.

"Watching you sleep," Noah said.

I shivered.

"You've got such an innocent little face, but you and I both know there's nothing innocent about you."

He disappeared only to reappear behind me. His breath was metallic, like ice on my neck. "I miss eating fruit the most. But you'll be a nice substitute. I bet your blood tastes like honey."

Focus. Feel. Smell. Do not fight your instincts.

He gripped my arms and pulled me to his chest. Fear-laced adrenaline pumped through me. I closed my eyes and jumped, hoping to throw Noah off balance just enough to loosen his ironclad hold.

My body propelled to the ceiling, knocking Noah into

the wall. I bared my fangs and hissed like a pissed-off cat. Then I dove straight down toward Noah.

"No!" Mr. Charles yelled. "Noah, don't! If you kill her, the elders will punish you," he warned.

"It'll be worth it," Noah said, dodging my assault. "Come on, tease. Can't you do better than that?"

I had no idea. This was all so new to me. I had spent my entire life avoiding the reality that I was a vampire. I had never worked on any of my skills other than hearing. Hell, if the flying was any indication, I didn't even know what skills I had.

Noah's laughter filled my head. I realized he was getting to me, trying to weaken me. I needed to concentrate. If he could figure out how to sharpen his powers over just a few days, then surely with a little focus I could do the same. After all, technically I had seventeen years' experience over him.

That's right. You are better, stronger, smarter. Stay in control. Focus.

I closed my eyes and began to ascend again. I would dip if I stopped concentrating, so I worked hard to stay in control. My senses opened up and suddenly I knew what Noah's next move was going to be. He darted toward me, and I moved to the left, never once opening my eyes.

He crashed into the wall, putting a hole in the plaster. "Bitch," he spat.

I ignored him and kept in focus. Surprisingly, I managed to stay in the air. I took a deep breath. "Do you miss breathing, Noah? Do you miss smelling fresh herbs and flowers, or maybe the smell of Twittany's cheap perfume?"

Noah growled and lunged again, but I deftly avoided his attack. His frustration and anger were tangible. And I could read him like a book, so I was ready when he dove for the butcher block, grabbed a knife, and chucked it at me.

I caught it and chucked it right back. It impaled him in the arm and pinned him to the wall.

His scream was so high-pitched, it burst the windows and broke my concentration. I opened my eyes and saw his eyes burn bright. He pulled the knife out, and his arm healed on the spot.

I felt myself falling slightly, and I struggled to regain my focus. But Noah saw the opportunity and pounced, bringing us both to the ground in a pile of shattered glass. He held the knife to my throat.

"What will happen to you when I bite your pretty little neck?" he asked, licking my throat.

I swallowed the bile as it rose. "I don't know." My voice was shaky. "Lucky for me, I'll never find out," I said, grabbing a large shard of glass and ramming it into his heart. Thank God the whole wooden stake thing was just a myth.

As the shard entered his chest, there was no shriek, only the flash of surprise in his eyes. His features softened back to the Noah I once knew, his eyes faded from red to blue. He sighed. His icy breath warmed, his tight, thick skin relaxed.

And then, in a puff of smoke, he turned to ash.

My heart was heavy. Now that Noah the monster was gone, I could mourn the death of Noah my friend.

felt hung over. Okay, I felt what I imagined a hangover would be like. My head throbbed, my stomach roiled, and even the smallest movements made the room spin.

And I was covered in Noah's ashes, which was starting to creep me out. I tried to stand, but my body was too weak. So I dragged myself out of the pile, the glass crushing beneath me, cutting into my legs as I moved.

"That was scary," Mr. Charles said, putting his arms beneath me and gently lifting me out of the debris.

I nodded. I couldn't stand, couldn't speak, couldn't get away.

"Your body needs to recuperate, and you need a

hemoshake." He sat me in a kitchen chair and opened the fridge. "If you promise to cooperate, I'll give you this."

I nodded. I had no choice. I had to do whatever I could to regain my strength.

He handed me the canned drink, I popped it open and pretended to take a big swallow. I wanted him to think I was cooperating. I was buying time—for what, I had no idea. "Were you feeding Noah? How did you keep him from killing you?"

"His master had control over him. He had no choice—at least he didn't at first. I guess when you didn't wear your amulet of protection, his desire for you outweighed his master's control," he said as he picked up the gun and pointed it at me. "That was amazing. You understand why I have to use this, right? After seeing what kind of powers you have, I can't take any chances that you'll use them against me. I don't want to hurt you, AJ, but I will if I have to."

I nodded, trying to buy some more time. "My amulet?"

"That necklace you've been wearing and those herbs. How did you know what spell to cast to protect yourself?" he asked.

"My grandmother," I lied. If I ever got out of this

mess, Aunt Doreen had some 'splainin' to do.

"I knew there was more to that story," he said with a laugh, like we were old friends meeting for coffee. "AJ, you should start to feel sleepy soon. I'm sorry, but I couldn't take the chance—so I drugged the hemoshake," he said.

I let my eyelids droop heavily and I nodded again. I slumped in the chair. He reached for me, steadying me with his arm around my shoulders. I grabbed his arm and sank my teeth, fangs and all, into his skin. I was careful to bite only. Though it was tempting to suck him free of his life-force and make him my slave.

"Aaaagh! You bit me?" he screamed, then dropped the gun and yanked his arm away to inspect his injury.

"Oh? Did I do that?"

I wasn't really sure how to react to the fact that I had just bitten a man on purpose. The smell of fresh blood sent my senses into overdrive. I salivated, then licked the blood droplets off my lips. I really hadn't given any thought to what might happen to him after the bite—or how my body would react. The only thing I could think about was getting the hell out of there.

I heard a gasp in the doorway.

"AJ?" Ryan said.

So much for keeping the family secret a secret.

Somehow I found the strength to stand and stumble to Ryan. He didn't pull away from me; I figured his not being repulsed was a good sign.

"I'll explain it all, but first we need to get out of here," I said as Mr. Charles stood and reached behind his back. "Now!"

A shot rang in the kitchen, and the door frame next to Ryan's head splintered.

Ryan yelled, grabbing my hand and pulling me into the living room. "Get out of the way!"

Staring down the barrel of the gun, Ryan faced Mr. Charles. He balanced himself on his right foot, pointed his right hand straight out, and closed his left eye. He looked like a one-eyed stork ninja.

What the hell was Ryan planning to do, wink Mr. Charles to death?

Suddenly, in a panicked whisper, Ryan began to chant in a language I had never heard before. As the words spilled from his mouth, the air grew static. The scar on my palm burned and glowed a bright orange with each word. Mr. Charles pulled the hammer back on the gun. Time stood still. Ryan continued his rushed chanting. As Mr. Charles aimed the gun toward Ryan—no way was he gonna miss this time—I squeezed my eyes shut, said a little prayer, and then there was a bright flash and a pop.

And silence.

I opened one eye, terrified that Ryan would be lying on the ground in a pool of blood. Instead, Mr. Charles had disappeared in a cloud of black smoke.

"Whoa," I said.

"Oops. Did I do that?" Ryan laughed nervously. "Guess we need to catch up a little."

Apparently, Aunt Doreen was not the only one who had some 'splainin' to do.

Chapter 25

A loud knock on the door was followed by Cody Littleton's voice. "Police! We have a warrant!"

The words were barely out of Cody's mouth before he and three other deputies barreled into the house.

"Kids, are y'all okay?" he asked.

"Yeah, just shaken up," I said.

"Where's Mr. Charles?"

I looked at Ryan, who smiled and shrugged.

"He just disappeared," I said.

"Yeah. One minute he was here, and the next—poof!" Ryan added.

"Where did he go?" Cody asked.

"I wish I knew," Ryan answered as we walked outside. He leaned over and whispered in my ear, "Seriously, I wish I knew. I have no idea where I sent him."

Cody used his radio to call the criminal investigation unit to come and start collecting evidence. "Let's get y'all to the station," he said. "Your parents are waiting for you."

The harsh fluorescent lights glared at us as we pushed through the glass double doors. An intern sat behind the front desk chewing on a pencil. His eyes went wide when he saw Cody bringing us in.

"The sheriff is waiting for you in room one," he said.

The solid metal doors down the hallway opened and our parents walked out. They rushed to us and wrapped us up in a group hug. "Are y'all okay?" they asked simultaneously.

"Yeah. We are. Mr. Charles went crazy. It was weird. He had a gun—"

My mom gasped.

"We're okay, Momma. See, still alive and kicking."

"Thank God. Let's go home, shower, and have Aunt Doreen fix us something warm and delicious. And discuss how I'm never letting you out of my sight again."

Sheriff Christopher took that moment to clear his

throat and announce his presence. "AJ, I sure am glad I didn't wait for you in your kitchen."

My cheeks blazed. "Sorry. I had to figure a few things out before I talked to you."

"You mean get your story straight?" he asked.

Rick stepped forward, wrapping his arm around my shoulders. "That's not very fair, Sheriff. She's just a kid, and this has been a really stressful week even by adult standards. Why don't you cut her a break?"

God, that felt good. Seriously. To have somebody, *anybody* support me unconditionally, no questions asked. What a concept. And what a change from earlier at his office.

I looked up at Rick and smiled. "Thanks."

Rick's dark brown eyes smiled back at me. "No problem, kiddo."

Mom pulled me into a huge hug. "I'm sorry, sweetheart. I should've listened to you."

It felt really good to have my momma back. "I'm sorry, too."

"When y'all are finished with your little *Brady Bunch* reunion show, I'd like to ask AJ a few questions. Ryan, you can go home; we're finished with you," Sheriff Christopher said.

"They're not going to arrest you?" I asked Ryan.

"No. The autopsy report showed that a snakebite killed him. I only punched him twice. I was just afraid you had come back after him with a baseball bat. Or a car. You were pretty pissed," Ryan said.

"So you thought you were protecting me," I said.

Ryan nodded.

"Can we wrap this up?" the sheriff asked impatiently. "I'd like to get this over with."

"You don't have to do this if you don't want to," Mom said.

"It's okay. I want to."

Ryan wrapped me up in a giant hug and I could feel the tension leave him. "Are you all right?" I asked.

"Yeah. I'm good now."

He pulled back, and we stared into each other's eyes for a moment. My heart hitched, and the knot in my belly moved to my throat.

Rick turned to my mom. "Liz, if you're okay with it, I'll stay here with AJ."

Ryan grabbed my hand and squeezed it. For what seemed like the hundredth time today, tears stung my eyes. I felt the words I wanted to say but couldn't, so I closed my eyes and whispered them in my head.

"Ouch!" Ryan said, grabbing his head right above his ear.

"What?" Rick asked.

"Nothing. Just the weirdest head pain. Intense," he said.

"Probably just stress. Let's go home and get you an aspirin," Mom said, leading him out the door.

As I watched them leave, I could've sworn I heard Ryan's voice in my head, telling me he loved me, too.

The sheriff led us down the hallway, past a couple of offices, and into a room that looked like it came right out of *Law & Order*.

The smell of burnt coffee filled the space. The sheriff waved his hand toward the table in the center of the room. Rick pulled out a chair for me, then sat next to me. We waited while Sheriff Christopher fixed himself a cup of that vile black liquid.

"Coffee?" he asked us.

"No, thank you," Rick answered. His accent was light, almost undetectable, unlike Aunt Doreen's thick, almost indecipherable burr.

"First things first," the sheriff said. "You're lucky I don't press charges for interfering with an investigation."

"Al, she's aware what she did was wrong. Cut the girl a

break and move on. For Christ's sake, she's seventeen and wanted to protect her brother," Rick said.

My brother. Ugh, how I hated those words. Ryan was no more my brother than the man in the moon.

"Darlin'," the sheriff said. "This stuff between you and your teacher is very serious. And I know it's gonna be a little embarrassing, and I apologize for that. But I need to know: Were you sleeping with your teacher?"

"Ew. No," I answered. "I mean, I thought he was hot until he went loco, but still no. He hugged me once. That's it. And there was nothing to the hug. It was a fatherly hug, not a creep-me-out hug." I wish it *had* creeped me out, though. If I had gotten the psycho vibe, we wouldn't be here right now.

"We collected some evidence from his classroom today that indicates he was obsessed with you—and that he thought you were some kind of 'chosen' vampire. Were you aware of that?" he asked.

"Not until I went over there this afternoon. He had this journal of his plans to gain my trust and how he even planned to get me suspended for cheating. If I had known *all that*, I never would have gone to his house. I thought he was a victim, too. I thought we should come to the police together. I trusted him. I thought he was my friend." I sobbed.

Rick draped his arm across the back of my chair and pulled me closer to him. "It's okay, honey. You're safe, and that's what matters."

"I need you to tell me what happened from start to finish," the sheriff said. "Don't leave any detail out. We need to figure out where Mr. Charles disappeared to."

"He mentioned something about clan elders and that they were waiting for him to bring me to them," I said.

"According to some of the emails we accessed from his computer at work, he was going to take you to some kind of vampire cult. Unfortunately for us, he didn't leave any detailed information about where this cult is located. And I'm sure the emails were sent from a dummy address. We're hopeful he left some information on his hard drive at the house. You're a lucky girl," the sheriff said. "Being the target of any cult is bad, but those folks who think they're vampires are especially dangerous because they're just not right in the head." He shook his head and laughed. "Vampires? Of all the things to believe in."

"We're all lucky," Rick said. "Come on, sweetheart. Let's get you home."

We got in the car and drove in silence for a few minutes. I was trying to be strong, but with everything that had happened this week, I felt more than a little overwhelmed.

Mr. Charles had known my secret because my own father led him to me.

And then there was the whole Ryan thing. He'd watched me bite Mr. Charles but it hadn't seemed to freak him out. Of course, why should he freak when he had the magic ninja stork move?

"I'm in the mood for a milk shake, how about you?" Rick asked as he pulled into Bumpers. "You know, I fell in love with your mother right here. She ordered a vanilla malt and won my heart."

I smiled. "I'm more of an orange cream slush girl, myself."

"Funny, so is Ryan."

He rolled down the window, punched the button, and placed our order.

"Are you okay?" he asked me, after the Bumpers girl wheeled our food to us on her roller skates.

"Yeah. I'm a little weak, and a little freaked. But I'm good." I took a long pull off my straw. The orange cream was cold and soothing and just what I needed.

"How are you and Ryan doing with this stepsibling thing? I know it's really hard, what your mom and I have done to the two of you. And I know you can't just turn off your feelings like a light switch."

This was so weird, talking about my not-so-sisterly feelings for my stepbrother with my stepfather. Seriously, I expected a call from Jerry Springer any minute now.

"We're coping. I mean, we've only been brother and sister for a week."

"And what a week! If your mom and I had realized our wedding would launch such a shit storm . . ."

"You would've just eloped," I said, laughing.

"Yeah. Probably. Your mom is the best thing to ever happen to me."

Funny. That's exactly how I felt about his son.

"I need a nap," I said as Rick pulled into the driveway. "I need to recover from all that drama."

Rick sighed. "Yeah, well, drama kind of comes with being a"—he paused, seeming to choose his words carefully—"Fraser. And you're officially a member of the family, so you might want to get used to it."

"We Ashes bring our share of drama to the table. It's in our nature."

Rick smiled as if he understood completely, which made a lot of sense considering that his son could shoot fireworks from his fingertips. I wonder if that was a genetic thing.

I liked Rick—a lot. I couldn't have asked for a better

stepfather. So it was gonna suck big fat pickles when he discovered our little secret. Even though they obviously had secrets of their own, when Rick finds out he's married to a vampire, he'll leave and take his kids with him. And then I won't even have Ryan as a brother.

The smell of pumpkin bread and coffee made my mouth water as we entered the kitchen. Mom was on the phone and Aunt Doreen was slicing the fresh baked bread.

"Hello, sweetheart," Rick whispered, kissing Mom on the cheek as she listened into the receiver intently, only voicing the occasional "mmhmm," "yes," and "I understand" until finally, "Thank you, Ms. Blanchard. I appreciate your call and I'll be sure to let her know. Good-bye."

"Hey, honey," Momma said to Rick as she hung up the phone. Then she walked over to me and wrapped me up. "So I've got some good news," she said, finally letting me go.

"I could use some of that."

Rick draped his arm around Mom's shoulders. They fit together like a puzzle. "That was Ms. Blanchard. She's been in touch with the police and knows everything. You've been cleared of the cheating and your suspension has been lifted."

Relief flooded me. "Really?"

"Really. She's in shock about Mr. Charles. She can't believe he was so deluded that he thought you were some vampire queen." Mom winked at me, and I stifled a giggle. "She said you might want to be prepared for some merciless teasing from the kids at school."

"I can handle the teasing. Maybe I'll even play along, with some vampire teeth and a tiara. I'm always looking for an excuse to wear a tiara, anyway."

And the good news was, I already had the fangs.

Chapter 26

I would say that I fell asleep fast, but honestly, I don't think my "nap" could be counted as sleep.

The dreams came immediately and they felt so real, so alive, that when I finally woke, I was more exhausted than before.

In the dreams, I saw Mr. Charles. He was with a man in a dark robe. His face was hidden but it was definitely a man. He was too broad-shouldered to be a woman. And he just had a very . . . male presence.

Anyway, Mr. Charles was handing the Serpentine Scrolls over to the man in the robe. There were other people standing in the shadows, but I couldn't see their faces, either.

I was there, too, only not physically. More like a fly on the wall. I could see everything happening, but nobody knew I was there.

Except for the man in the robe. I knew he could see me because he turned and looked right at me. Shadows covered his face, but I saw his eyes. Electric blue. Sharp. All-knowing.

He held up his hand with his palm facing out. He was showing me his mark, the backward S on his palm that matched mine.

I jolted awake when my palm began to burn. I removed the bandage that I had so carefully kept in place and looked at my mark.

They had branded me. And now they were tracking me.

I couldn't explain the sense of violation I felt. The invasion was personal, like a hidden video camera in your bedroom. Or worse, in your bathroom.

It was past time to talk to Mom. Obviously I was in over my head and needed some major guidance—guidance I had thought I was getting from Mr. Charles.

He had said my father was responsible for him tracking me down. Did that mean Mr. Charles was his human servant? I'd read about those before, but I thought that most

281

vampire clans nowadays didn't condone using humans like that. Of course, if half of what I'd read about the Serpentines was true . . .

Yeah, they probably wouldn't have any problem with controlling humans on a whim. Especially a human like Mr. Charles, who seemed to be obsessed with everything vampire. He wanted immortality, and he more or less sold his soul to get it. The other side of this issue was that in order for a vampire to have a human servant, he had to have a massive amount of power. The kind of power that could only be developed over centuries of practice and control. And that was a very scary thought. Even scarier was the thought that *that vampire* could be my father.

I walked downstairs to find Mom, Rick, and Aunt Doreen rounding up the kids. Ryan was sitting on the couch, the twins were in the oversized leather chair whispering (which meant they were totally conspiring against Rayden again), Rayden was walking in with a wary look on his face, and Oz trailed behind him, wearing a chocolate milk mustache and pumpkin bread crumbs.

"Am I missing a family meeting?" I asked Mom as I hit the last step.

"There you are. I was just about to come and get you. I think this is the first time we've all been under the same roof at the same time since the wedding," she said. "Come on in and sit."

I had a bad feeling about this gathering. We were either gonna get a lecture, get some bad news, or they were gonna offer to take us on their honeymoon, just like Mike and Carol Brady did. I'd take bad news over their honeymoon anytime, thank-you-very-much.

I sat on the other end of the couch, careful not to come in contact with Ryan, even though I felt pulled to him like a magnet. When was I gonna get over this stupid attraction?

Aunt Doreen took a seat on the ottoman with the pretty pink square she was knitting while Mom and Rick continued to stand.

"This has been a very traumatic week," Mom said. "First with the wedding, then with Noah's death, then Ryan and AJ being accused of cheating, and the whole Mr. Charles drama . . . and I'm not even counting the adjustment to living together, which is its own kind of trauma."

"Liz and I hate to add to the commotion, but we have something we need to discuss with you guys. It's very important and it's going to change our family dynamic in a big way," Rick said.

"This isn't going to be easy for y'all to hear. It's important that you understand there's a bigger picture and what we're about to tell you is a key component to that picture. It's going to seem unbelievable at first, but I know you'll all be open and receptive to it," Mom said.

"It's high past time for complete honesty," Rick said.

"That's the truth of it," Aunt Doreen mumbled.

"So we're going to start with our big secret," Mom said.

Here it was. The moment of truth. Mom was going to jump out of the vampire closet. And even though Ryan saw me fang Mr. Charles, I still wasn't 100 percent sure that he was ready for the word "vampire."

And what would Rick say?

"I'm pregnant."

I'm sorry? Pregnant? Really?

"Ewwwww," Rayden said. "That means that—"

"Thank you, Captain Obvious," Ryan said, interrupting Ray before he could finish his sentence. "I think we all know what that means."

"It means that as a family, we have a lot to work out," Mom said. "And it's more than just bringing a new baby into the world."

"So, Rick knows about our family, um, genetics?" I asked.

"I do," Rick said.

All three Fraser boys looked at their father. "Huh?" Rayden and Oz asked.

Interesting. Sure, he was okay with being married to a vampire, but would he really be okay with having a vampire kid?

"Okay, I'm not sure of the best way to do this," Mom said, looking at Rick. "We're not the only ones in the family who have some special genetics that could be passed onto the baby."

Ana and Ainsley giggled a little, and all the brothers shot each other the same, worried glance.

A loud sigh escaped from Aunt Doreen. I glanced over to see her knitting furiously fast with a look of frustration on her face. "By the goddess, what yer mum is trying to say is that we're Frieceadan. I'm a witch. The lads are warlocks," she said. "I've been smellin' evil since Monday morning but couldn't place it. So I've been trying to protect you with herbs and amulets. You're really not that stinky." She winked.

"That explains a lot," I said. "And Ryan's fingertip fireworks?"

"Ryan saved you today because that's our destiny. Don't think for a second it was coincidence that brought our families together," Aunt Doreen said. "You should know that by now, after all that research ye've been doin'."

"I may have the Frieceadan powers," Ryan mumbled, "but I still can't find my Frieceadan mark."

"It'll come, lad. Dinna fash yerself," Aunt D assured him.

Maybe I should be more surprised by the revelation, but I guess it was more of a confirmation for me, since I actually witnessed Ryan's ability firsthand today.

The girls just rolled their eyes at the announcement. "Like, duh," the twins said. "We've known since forever. You guys are slow."

Aunt Doreen laughed. "The weans always know. They're so much more open to special abilities."

I noticed that her hands were still on her temples and the knitting needles were still knitting.

And then, suddenly, it all made sense.

"No way. You know what this means?" I asked Mom. "I may be a key holder, but *you* are the chosen one."

Chapter 27

"Wait a minute," Ryan said. "Chosen what? You don't even seemed surprised that we're, um, not normal."

I laughed so hard that my belly hurt. Not normal? That was rich. I'd give anything to be a witch. People were much more accepting of witches. But vampires? Who wanted a bloodsucking fiend as their BFF? Or girlfriend? Or stepsister?

"Of course I'm not surprised, after your little fireworks display earlier. The fact that you're Frieceadan explains everything—hang on a second," I said. "Didn't you see me bite Mr. Charles?"

"You bit Mr. Charles?" My mom gasped.

"Yeah. I did. I was totally freaked and he was trying to drug me. I didn't do anything else," I said, trying to reassure her that I had not sucked his body dry and therefore was sure I hadn't turned him. Well, mostly sure.

"I saw you bite him," Ryan said. "I probably would've bitten him to get away, too."

"But you didn't see my—" My what? Fang-bearing levitation? My knife-throwing midair fight against the undead Noah?

Suddenly I had restless leg syndrome as adrenaline and anxiety shot through me. I stood and paced while everyone watched me with cautious interest. I thought he had seen me as Vampira and accepted that about me. But I had been wrong. Telling him was going to be harder than I thought.

"See, I've been doing some family research this week. I wasn't calling it family research, but that's what it was," I said.

"Mr. Charles isn't a genealogy expert. Why would you go to him for help?" Ryan asked.

I looked over at Mom. "Go ahead," she said. "It will probably be better coming from you, anyway."

"Mr. Charles is an expert in occult mythology. And that's what I was researching. I was using my thesis as the reason, but really it was to find out more about my family history because after Noah died, I thought maybe I had killed him."

Oz and Rayden were staring at me in open-mouthed wonder, but Ryan was still confused. "You couldn't have killed Noah—unless you're a snake," Ryan said.

I raised my eyebrows and just looked at him.

"You made the snake bite him?" Ryan asked. "I must be really thick, because I'm just not getting it."

"No. I thought *I* bit him. I was so angry that night, and I woke up with no memory and covered in blood. I thought maybe I had blacked out and gone back to Noah and lost control . . ."

The boys all silently stared as I paced. I closed my eyes and sighed.

"What I'm trying to say is, I'm, *we're* vampires. And I found out this week that my backward-S birthmark is actually a mark of our clan. We're not just vampires, we're Serpentines."

"*Whoa*. And I thought *we* were freaks," Rayden said.

"Totally cool," Oz added. "Can y'all show me your fangs?" he asked the twins.

Ana and Ainsley looked at each other with a twinkle in their eyes. They smiled a big toothy grin for their stepbrothers, showing all their teeth . . . including their fangs.

"Awesome," Oz and Rayden both said.

"Can we go outside and show them some of our tricks?" Rayden asked.

"Yes, that's fine. Just don't be careless. The family rules don't change, okay?" Rick said.

The kids left and Aunt Doreen packed up her knitting and followed them. "I think it might be best if I keep an eye on the weans. We canna leave them unsupervised for too long. Rayden tends to get a little slipshod when he's showin' off." She turned to me and winked. "I knew ye were special, lass."

Ryan sat stiff and stoic. He hadn't looked at me since I confessed my secret. It was like I had just sliced open a vein and was waiting to see if he would save me or leave me to die. And the waiting made my heart hurt. It had been easier when I thought he'd seen me in vampire mode and accepted me despite my fangs.

"AJ, you said something about me being the chosen one. What did you mean?" Mom asked, cutting through the thick silence in the room.

"Mr. Charles thought I was a key holder. The prophecy said that a child would be born to a Frieceadan Warlock and a former member of the Serpentine Clan. That child would bear the marks of both clans and the baby's blood would be the anti-serum to the Serpentine Venom. That child would render the Serpentines powerless, which is why they tried to eradicate the Frieceadans all those years ago.

"I'd assumed the prophecy meant a pure-blooded Serpentine. But I don't think that's the case. You bear the mark of the clan and you're pregnant by a Frieceadan Warlock. Momma, I think your baby is the prophesied child."

Momma looked at Rick, and he wrapped her into a hug. "What did Mr. Charles want from you exactly?" Mom asked.

"I'm not sure. He called me a key holder. He said the clan elders needed me to get their hands on the runes. They believe the runes can be used to time travel."

"If what you say is true, then fate really did bring our families together," Rick said, planting a light kiss on Mom's forehead. "I knew we were connected."

I glanced over at Ryan to gauge his reaction. He stood, walked over to me, and pulled my hair away from my neck to inspect my birthmark.

"What do you think they wanted to do with the runes?" he asked.

Chills followed the path his finger traced along my birthmark. "I think they planned to go back in time and change the future. They crave power and domination. They want to rule the world," I said, taking his hand in mine. "But we have a distinct advantage. They don't know you're Frieceadan. And we have to keep it that way."

"I guess we were fated to be together, too. Just not like we had once thought," Ryan said.

"We have to protect the family, Ryan. We could all be in a lot of danger," I said. "Mom, I left something out that you need to know."

"What's that?"

"Mr. Charles said that Dad is the one behind all of this. I'm afraid since Mr. Charles is no longer around to do his dirty work—"

"That Clive Ashe will come to take care of things himself," Mom said.

"That's not all. There's another vampire out there. I know you said it was a snakebite that killed Noah, but Mom"—I hesitated—"Noah was turned into a dichamp. He was after me. Stalked me. Threatened to feed on you and the twins if I told anyone. He couldn't touch me, thanks to the amulet Aunt D gave me, but I didn't know that at the time and I was terrified that if I came to you,

I'd be signing your death warrant. I'm sorry."

"Oh, honey." Momma pulled away from Rick and hugged me. "I'm sorry, too. I can't imagine how scary that was for you. And to handle it all by yourself." She choked up a little. "This was such a stressful week. What a way to start out as a family," she said, releasing me from her death-grip hug. "If we can survive this week, I think we can survive anything."

"Now what?" Ryan asked.

"We need to find out everything we can about our two families. The Serpentines want those runes, which means either they know or suspect that the Frieceadans are still around. They have to make sure that the chosen one and a Frieceadan don't hook up, which has already happened, but they don't know that," I said.

"They also think you can give them something—you being a key holder and all," Ryan said.

My heart shifted and kicked up a notch. "You're okay with me being a vampire?" I asked.

"You're family," he said. "And in our world, family is everything."

"We'll call Tave tomorrow. I have a feeling we're going to need her help," Mom said.

"You won't have to call her. Somehow we're still

connected. She'll be here for breakfast." I grinned.

Mom and Rick both smiled. "That went much better than we expected," Momma said.

"Well, it helps that you guys are much freakier than we are," Rick said.

"I'll show you freak," Mom replied with a wink.

"Ew. Yuck. Y'all go somewhere else with that, please," I said. "And Momma, be careful. We don't want them figuring this stuff out before my baby sister is born."

"Brother. Your mom's a Fraser now and we only have boys," Ryan said.

Our parents left the room, holding hands and being generally too cute to stomach.

I watched them leave, envious of their affection. I wanted that back. With Ryan. But that wasn't going to happen. And I had to learn to live with it.

This had been the longest week ever. I had given up my boyfriend for a new brother. I had been stalked by a dichamp, been chased by a crazy teacher, and discovered I'm a descendant of an evil clan of vampires. And let's not forget that I am apparently some sort of key to a time-traveling device.

Not to mention my two best friends are still at odds with each other and I'm stuck in the middle. Being the duct tape holding our tripod together wasn't going to be easy. Especially since I have to keep even more secrets from them.

I sighed, and Ryan wrapped me up in a hug. For a moment, I let myself forget everything and just feel. I still wanted him, and everything in my soul ached for his touch.

But that wasn't our destiny.

"We can do this," he said. "In twenty years, we'll be spending Christmas with our families and we'll all laugh about the time we were almost a Mississippi cliché," Ryan said.

"Do you think so? Really?" I asked, wanting to believe him but not sure I could.

"I know so, because we don't have a choice. Fate has something else in mind for us. It won't be easy, but this is bigger than we are. Now, come on, Sis. Let me show you how I managed to create and hang all those campaign posters in one night."

"That explains it! And you used your ninja stork ju-ju to remove them, too, didn't you?"

"Guilty."

"I think I'm gonna like this brother with benefits thing."

"Okay, that sounded a little incestuous and creepy. How about we just call me Captain Awesome and move on."

"Captain Ego is more like it. You keep that up and getting over you will be a painless snap."

Okay, maybe not painless, but now that I knew we were meant to protect our family together, maybe it would make it easier to move on. Because it was for the greater good and all that. It was fate.

Ryan smiled at me again, and my heart flipped, just as it always did. Okay, so maybe bowing to our destinies was going to be a little harder than I thought.

I grimaced.

Bite me, Fate. You suck.

Acknowledgments

I'll admit it: My acknowledgment page could be a chapter all by itself. There are so many people who have touched my life since I started this journey who have made me not only a better writer but a better person. I'll try to be brief.

Deidre Knight—your name says it all. You are my knight in shining agentry. You have never once wavered in your support or belief in me. To me, you are better than chocolate. No writer should be without an agent or a friend like you. I'm lucky to have you as both.

Maria Geraci—you are the first critique partner to stick and you turned into my best friend. Who knew I had a Cuban spitfire sister who could "show-out" like nobody's business?

Louisa Edwards—my second critique partner to stick. I am so lucky to have you in my life. You have the best eye and one of the biggest hearts I know. Plus, you are the queen of commas. (Does a comma belong after "plus"? I hope so. I mean, I paused when I read it in my head, so surely a comma belongs there. . . .)

Kristin Daly—I was terrified of my first editorial letter. But once I read it and realized how in sync we were, I knew I was in good hands. You took the bones of a good story and added the flesh. And I can't thank you enough. I feel very blessed to count you as my first editor.

Megan Geraci—thank you so much for being my beta reader and letting me know when I wrote something that "only old people would say." I'm probably showing my age when I tell you I think you rock like Adam Ant.

Beach Bunnies—you know who you are and why I love you. Thank you for everything.

And last but not least, to my family. I am so grateful that my boys aren't embarrassed to call me Mom (most of the time) and that my husband tolerates my fits of emotional instability when the words just won't come. Mark Francis, you are my MF. 897.

AJ's story continues in

Love Sucks!

By Melissa Francis

My mother's baby shower.

Okay, this is horrifying news on many levels. First of all, I'm seventeen. I know how she got pregnant. And let me just say—ew. Seriously, ew.

It's been five months since the big baby announcement. Five long months. In that time, I've managed to discover a lot more about the warlock side of my blended family, thanks to Ryan's aunt Doreen. Though I still have a lot to learn about both the Frieceadan warlocks as well as the Serpentine vampires. I'm deathly afraid that if the Serpentines realize my mom is pregnant with a warlock's child, all undead hell is going to break loose.

And let me just say, I'm in no mood for vampire wars.

So as I sit in the living room with two dozen of Valley Springs' finest women, oohing and ahhing over the sweetest little baby gifts you could ever imagine, all I seem to think about is evil vampires, good warlocks, and a possible paranormal apocalypse.

Something is *really* not right with this picture.

Aunt Doreen passed me the latest opened gift—a lovely little layette in mint green with a fuzzy baby bunny on the breast. When would my hell be over?

The ladies all stood and I realized the shower was coming to an end. Finally.

As the crew of crooning women stood to start their farewells, a storm of testosterone entered the room and headed straight for the remainder of the pretty lemon cake. My stepdad, Rick, and my two younger stepbrothers, Oz and Rayden, each cut themselves a slice big enough to feed a third-world country. Ryan came in shortly after and did the same.

We made eye contact and I fought the old squiggly feeling in my belly when his dark-chocolate gaze caught mine.

Suddenly the kitchen door slammed open and Ainsley called my name as she rushed into the house. Her voice was panicked.

"AJ!"

"Living room," I said.

Ainsley's long, wheat-colored ponytail swung like a mane behind her head as she rushed into the room.

"Something's not right with Ana," she said in a panic.

Oz and Rayden stopped midchew.

"We didn't do anything," Rayden said, his eyes wide. "I swear."

Ainsley turned toward them. "This isn't about your sad spell-casting attempt to turn her into a Sasquatch. When she woke up this morning with pit hair longer than her ponytail, Aunt D fixed her right up. But don't think she won't get y'all back. If we can find her again."

"Find her? What's going on?" I asked.

"Tryouts were today, right?" Ainsley said in a rush. "Well, we were doing the routine we always do with the gymnastics bit? You know, with the midair acrobatics that impress everyone?"

I nodded. She and Ana had no issues using their super skills to jump just a little bit higher than everyone else and add one extra twist or flip to their routine.

"Well, something went wrong. Ana didn't land well— which just isn't possible. Seriously, she's like a cat. She never misses her landings. Ever!" Ainsley said.

"Then what happened?" I asked.

"Her ankle snapped. I heard it. Of course, it was

already starting to heal by the time everyone got over to her. But the damage was already done. She had fallen. During *tryouts*. And everyone heard her bone crack."

"Well, Malia knows what kind of cheerleader Ana is. She'll make the team."

"That's just it—she didn't. They wrapped her ankle, and she faked a call to Mom to take her to the doctor. But they all think her ankle is broken, which means she'd have to sit out the season. So she didn't make the team. And, of course, she's totally pouting and blaming Malia," Ainsley said. "She took off after tryouts."

I sighed. "Where is she?" I asked. "Listen, I know you're communicating with her right now. Tell me where she is and I'll go get her."

"Hang on, let me see if I can get her to tell me."

Ainsley closed her eyes and concentrated. Then her eyes went wide. "She's running. Something isn't right. Oh my God." Ainsley gasped. "She's broken our connection."

A familiar sense of dread tickled my spine. "There's more. What is it?"

Ainsley looked into my eyes and, with a shaky voice, said, "Right before she vanished, her last thought was, *Oh my God! Mr. Charles.*"